HOOP MAGIC

Also by Eric Howling
in the Lorimer Sports Stories series

Kayak Combat
Drive

HOOP MAGIC
Eric Howling

James Lorimer & Company Ltd., Publishers
Toronto

James Lorimer & Company Ltd., Publishers acknowledges the support of the Ontario Arts Council. We acknowledge the financial support of the Government of Canada through the Canada Book Fund for our publishing activities. We acknowledge the support of the Canada Council for the Arts which last year invested $24.3 million in writing and publishing throughout Canada. We acknowledge the Government of Ontario through the Ontario Media Development Corporation's Ontario Book Initiative.

Cover design: Tyler Cleroux
Cover image: iStock

Library and Archives Canada Cataloguing in Publication

Howling, Eric, 1956-, author
Hoop magic / Eric Howling.

(Sports stories)
Issued in print and electronic formats.
ISBN 978-1-4594-0524-0 (bound).--ISBN 978-1-4594-0525-7 (pbk.).

I. Title. II. Series: Sports stories (Toronto, Ont.)

PS8615.O9485H66 2013   jC813'.6   C2013-904185-0   C2013-904186-9

James Lorimer & Company Ltd.,
Publishers
317 Adelaide Street West, Suite 1002
Toronto, ON, Canada
M5V 1P9
www.lorimer.ca

Distributed in the United States by:
Orca Book Publishers
P.O. Box 468
Custer, WA USA
98240-0468

Printed and bound in Canada.
Manufactured by Friesens Corporation in Altona, Manitoba, Canada in August 2013.
Job #87604

For Julie

CONTENTS

1 HOME COURT

Orlando stood alone on his driveway and stared at the basket ten feet above him. The net was old and tattered from thousands of shots. The backboard was scuffed by outside jumpers banked off its clear glass surface. White chalk markings outlining the key were drawn on the black pavement beneath him.

But this was no ordinary home basketball court. To Orlando it was the arena where the NBA's Toronto Raptors played in front of 18,000 screaming fans. Orlando shut his eyes. He could see the TV cameras and the giant Jumbotron screen with his face on it. He could smell the buttered popcorn the spectators were eating. And most of all he could hear the crowd chanting his name: O-R-L-A-N-D-O! O-R-L-A-N-D-O! He liked the sound of that.

He cradled the ball in the crook of his arm and ran his fingers over its smooth, pebbled surface. His legs felt strong, ready to spring into action. But still Orlando, in his new white high-tops, grey sweatpants, and blue hoodie, stayed frozen in place. He could hear the voice of the announcer boom from the loudspeakers, "Starting at guard, at five-foot-two from Evergreen Junior High, the small man with the big shot, Orlando-o-o-o-o O'Malleeeey!" Now the crowd was on its feet giving him a standing ovation.

Orlando zipped up his hoodie. The sun had long since set and a cold September breeze was blowing off Lake Ontario across the rooftops of Kingston. A single bright light shone down from the top of the garage, casting a ghostly white glow over the driveway. Orlando had told his dad that he needed the floodlight. That there was no way he was going to get better without being able to practice long after it was dark. Orlando knew he could get pretty much what he wanted from his dad and mom. New BMX bike — check. New skateboard — check. They were both professors at nearby Queen's University and felt guilty about the long hours they spent at work, not at home. To get the latest gear all Orlando had to do was ask.

He didn't mind taking advantage of them, though. He thought he deserved it. After all, he was the one who had been adopted from Haiti. He was the one whose birth parents had been so poor they couldn't afford to feed him and stuck him in an orphanage. He was the one who had always been small. The one who was never going to hit a growth spurt like people kept telling him he would.

He was still extra short, especially when he stood beside his sister, Megan, who did sprout up last summer. Now when they measured back-to-back she was six inches taller. This really bugged Orlando because they were both exactly the same age! This fact confused a lot of people, especially their teachers when he and Megan had gone to the same school. They'd look at Orlando, then look at Megan, then back at Orlando and ask, "How can you both be fourteen?" Orlando would then have to go into a long explanation of how he was adopted and his sister wasn't. This year, Orlando had told his parents that he was tired of teachers asking him so many questions and he wanted to go to a different school from Megan. He got what he wanted, but being split up hadn't made everything easier. Now he was the new kid at school and didn't know anyone.

But being adopted and having a tall sister who was the same age weren't the only things that confused people. There was something bigger. Something that made people stare. His parents and sister all had blond hair, blue eyes, and white skin, while Orlando had black hair, dark brown eyes, and skin the colour of chocolate. This wasn't a big deal, though. To Orlando they were just Mom, Dad and Megan.

Orlando stared up at the imaginary scoreboard. There was under a minute left to play. The Raptors trailed by a single point. The clock ticked down with just thirty seconds left. The coach called a time-out and the whistle blew. "O'Malley!" he barked, "You're in!" Orlando pictured himself leaping off the bench and taking the in-bounds pass.

Finally Orlando's new Nike kicks started to move. He dribbled the ball across the driveway and continued to call the action. But now he wasn't just thinking it to himself, he was announcing the play-by-play out loud.

"O'MALLEY'S GOT THE BALL AT THE TOP OF THE KEY. HE'S BEING CLOSELY GUARDED BY THEIR BIG MAN, BUT HIS DRIBBLING SKILLS ARE NO MATCH FOR THE TALL DEFENDER. THE CLOCK TICKS DOWN TO TEN SECONDS. IT'S GO TIME. O'MALLEY TURNS TO FACE THE BASKET. THE DEFENDER'S ARMS REACH HIGH IN THE AIR TO BLOCK A POSSIBLE SHOT. JUST EIGHT SECONDS LEFT. O'MALLEY SCOOTS UNDER AND DRIVES THE LANE. HE CROSSES OVER FROM HIS LEFT HAND TO HIS RIGHT AND BEATS THE LAST OPPOSING PLAYER. ONLY FOUR SECONDS LEFT! HIS POWERFUL LEGS TAKE OFF FROM THE COURT AND HE SAILS THROUGH THE AIR LAYING THE BALL SOFTLY OFF THE BACKBOARD AND INTO THE NET AS THE BUZZER GOES OFF! THE GAME IS OVER. HE'S DONE IT AGAIN! THE CROWD GOES CRAZY! O'MALLEY IS MOBBED BY HIS TEAMMATES!"

Suddenly the front door of his house swung open. "Time to finish your homework and go to bed," his mom called. "You've got a big day tomorrow and you need your sleep."

Orlando knew tomorrow was special. It was the

tryout for the basketball team at Evergreen Junior High. Orlando had never played on a team before. Not a community team. Not even an elementary-school team. He'd always thought he was too small. The only place he'd ever played was right here on his driveway. Sometimes his friends from the neighbourhood would come over to play twenty-one, but mainly he just shot hoops by himself. Now he had a chance to prove he was good enough. And he thought he was plenty good. That's why he needed to squeeze in every last minute of practice. If he didn't make it, he'd know it was only because of his size.

Orlando's shadow darted across the driveway. He made a few more dribbles, faked to the left, and took one last shot. The ball hit the rim with a clang and fell harmlessly to the ground. *Man, that should have gone in!* he said to himself and went inside.

★★★

Orlando finished the last question of his homework assignment, put his pencil down on the white Ikea desk, and closed the cover of his *Science 8* textbook. His gaze slowly panned the bedroom. The walls were covered with posters of his favourite NBA stars — LeBron James, Dwyane Wade, Kobe Bryant, Steve Nash. They were all pictured in mid-flight doing monster jams or hitting long jumpers from way outside. In the corner next to a pile of dirty shirts and socks ready for the laundry stood a three-foot-high plastic basketball net, left over from when Orlando was a kid. Beneath the bright red hoop was a matching red garbage bin filled with round, scrunched-up pieces of paper that Orlando had shot, pretending they were balls. At least he didn't miss any of those shots. On the other wall was a big map of the world from *National Geographic* magazine. Orlando had put blue pushpins in all the countries he wanted to visit one day, including Haiti. He thought he'd better check out where he had come from.

Orlando turned off the desk lamp. Now the bedroom was dark except for the glow from the screen of his computer. He knew he was also supposed to shut that down, but tonight was no ordinary night. It was a game night.

He placed the thin, silver laptop on his bed and grabbed his headphones so his mom and dad wouldn't hear what he was up to. He had asked for the phones last Christmas without telling his parents what he was secretly going to use them for. They probably thought he was listening to music. Not that he didn't like listening to tunes, but he liked listening to basketball games more. Orlando slid into bed, pulled the big metallic blue phones over his ears and plugged in. A couple of seconds later he was online and clicking on his favourite bookmark: HOOP Radio. That was the station that broadcast all the Toronto Raptors games and gave you every scrap of inside basketball news on the Raps that you ever wanted to know. How many players did they have? (Seventeen.) How many countries did they come from? (Six.) How tall was their centre? (Seven feet.) Orlando drank it all in like he was guzzling a bottle of Gatorade.

"You're tuned into HOOP Radio: the basketball station where you get to listen to all hoops, all the time. Whether you're catching the game in a car or listening before you go to sleep without your parents knowing, we want to thank all you fans for joining the Todd and Ted show." Orlando smiled. He felt like the announcers were talking right to him.

Tonight the Raptors were in Chicago to play the Bulls. Orlando knew the Raptors would have their hands full trying to stop Derek Rose, the speedy NBA all-star. By the time he crawled into bed the game was in the fourth quarter and almost over. It was all Bulls. They were rolling over the Raptors and were up by twenty points. Rose was having a big night and had scored forty-two points. The guy was unstoppable.

"Here comes Rose again slashing into the paint looking for another bucket. He takes off ten feet from the hoop skying right over the Raptors defender and slams the rock through the rim for the monster jam. Wow! How about that Todd!"

Orlando's face broke into a big toothy grin. He loved how the two guys behind the microphone talked. How their voices went up when there was a great play and how they went down when something bad happened.

It was like listening to a roller coaster of basketball emotions. He thought that being a sports announcer like Todd and Ted must be the most awesome job in the world. Travelling to all the big cities in North America like New York, Miami and Los Angeles — then sitting right next to the team benches and watching all the superstar NBA players race by on the court. Orlando didn't have to think twice about what he wanted to be when he got bigger, or at least older.

"Not a good night for the Raptors, but maybe they'll have better luck in two days when they tip off against the Boston Celtics in Beantown. And speaking of luck, don't forget to enter our big Courtside Contest, where one lucky fan will get to join Todd and me as we announce a Raptors game from right here at courtside."

Wow, Orlando thought. It sounded like the greatest contest ever. A chance to go to Toronto and watch a Raptors game live with Todd and Ted? *Man, that would be sick!*

Orlando couldn't wait to enter. He found the contest entry form on the HOOP website and typed in his name. Now all he had to do was cross his fingers and wait. He decided not to tell his mom or dad, because he didn't think it mattered much. After all, what were the chances of him winning?

2 THE BUBBLE

Tick. Orlando felt like he was in a time warp. *Tick.* Was it just his imagination or was the clock on the classroom wall moving slower than usual? *Tick.* He was supposed to be concentrating on his math teacher, Mr. Krinski, who was explaining the basics of algebra, but he kept looking over at the small hand to see another minute tick by in slow motion. Every sixty seconds seemed to take 120 seconds to pass. At least he was learning how to multiply by two.

Orlando sat fidgeting in his seat. His left leg bounced up and down like a basketball while the eraser end of his pencil tapped on the desk like a woodpecker drumming on a tree. If he wasn't careful he was going to use up all his energy before the tryout even started. Finally, the three-thirty bell sounded and Orlando bolted from his seat.

"Where's the fire, Mr. O'Malley?" Mr. Krinski asked, standing by the door at the front of the class. He was tall, thin, and wore a dark brown jacket that matched the colour of his hair and moustache. Arms crossed, he stared down at Orlando through black-rimmed glasses.

"I don't want to be late for the basketball tryout. The coach wouldn't like that."

"No, I'm sure he wouldn't, but I think you'll beat him there," Mr. Krinski said doing his best not to smile.

Orlando raced down the hall toward the gym with his backpack flying behind him. He zigzagged around a group of girls who were hanging out by their lockers, but then he hit a roadblock. A chain of five boys was spread across the hallway. To Orlando they were walking way too slowly and taking up way too much room. How could anyone get by?

"Out of my way!" Orlando shouted, trying to push his way through the human wall.

"What have we got here, Pete?" one of the boys said as he blocked Orlando's path.

"Looks like someone's on his way to basketball tryout, Keegan," Pete said. "Hey Cooper and Vijay, should we let Pint-sized pass?"

"Maybe we should, Davis, he could be better than all five of us put together." All the boys broke into laughter and fist-bumped each other.

"Why don't you take up space somewhere else?" Orlando said, frustrated at being picked on for his size.

"Like in the gym?" Pete asked.

"Yeah, if you even know where that is!" Orlando mocked.

"We have a rough idea." Vijay nodded.

Orlando spotted a hole in the human wall and darted for it. "Later, losers!"

The next thing Orlando knew he was tripping over an outstretched foot and sprawling on the hard tiled floor.

"Not so fast, Speedy," a voice from behind said.

Orlando picked himself up and raced toward the gym, never once looking back to see the laughing faces. Gasping for breath, he pushed open the door to the change room. He scanned the rows of tall, grey lockers and could only spot one that was empty — right next to Zack Jackson's! Zack was pulling a T-shirt from his locker. He then sat down to lace up his kicks.

Being a new kid at school, Orlando wasn't sure who would be at the tryout except for one, and that was Zack. He didn't know him, but he had sure heard about him. Even though Zack was only in grade eight, he was already the tallest boy at Evergreen Junior High. He even looked down on most of the teachers! Orlando never saw Zack hanging around with the other guys, though. He seemed a bit of a loner. In the cafeteria at lunchtime he'd eat by himself, and when Orlando walked by the gym before or after school, he'd see Zack shooting baskets all by himself. Orlando had heard the rumours about Zack's dad. How he used to argue with his mom and three years ago had driven away from home one night promising to come back to see Zack, but never did. Orlando figured Zack just needed time alone to think about it.

Orlando waited a few seconds to calm down, then walked over and stood in front of Evergreen's best player. "You're Zack Jackson!"

Zack ran his long fingers through his blond hair and nodded. "And who are you?"

"Orlando."

"Well, good luck out there, Orlando," Zack said, still sitting on the bench.

Orlando didn't think Zack seemed so tall. Then he stood up. Way, way up. Orlando had no idea how he was going to guard a giant like Zack.

Orlando started to put on his basketball gear. The locker room was so quiet you could hear a ball drop. Usually before gym class there was a lot of noisy joking going on between the guys. This afternoon it seemed everyone was nervous about the tryout and nobody was saying a word. Today, friends became competitors. Orlando finished putting on his white T-shirt and blue shorts, and laced up his high-tops. He took a deep breath and walked out onto the court.

The gym was still only half full. Orlando wondered whether everyone had arrived yet. He looked around and saw each player dressed in a different-coloured shirt. Red, blue, orange, yellow, black, grey, purple . . . every shade but one. Nobody would be wearing Eagle green-and-gold until the team was picked. The players continued to warm up by themselves. The sound of bouncing balls echoed through the gym. Most of the guys were shooting at the basket from different points on the court — top of the key, low post, deep in the corner. More shots were missing than dropping.

Sizing up the competition, Orlando thought he'd have a good chance of making the team if no one else showed up. Only Zack and a few of the others looked like they could match his skills. That thought changed in a flash when the locker-room door swung open and five boys ran onto the court dribbling like pros. These guys were good. Orlando realized they looked familiar. They were the same five guys he had mouthed off to in the hall!

How was I supposed to know they'd be here? Orlando dribbled to the other end of the gym, keeping his distance from Pete, Keegan, Cooper, Vijay, and Davis.

Five minutes later the whistle blew. "Let's bring it in!" Coach yelled across the gym.

Orlando picked up his ball and jogged in the direction of the booming voice. He had been so busy shooting hoops and staying clear of the other guys that he hadn't noticed the coach come out of the teachers' locker room. Standing in front of him with a whistle hanging around his neck was Mr. Krinski! He wore a green track suit with a gold flying eagle on the front, and a serious look on his face. His brown hair was mussed from pulling on the sweatshirt and one of his shoelaces was untied. Orlando couldn't believe this was the well-dressed teacher he'd just seen in math class.

"Welcome to the men's basketball tryout gentlemen," Coach Krinski said as he surveyed Orlando and the other boys. "I'll warn you right up front that making this team isn't going to be easy. There'll be a lot of sweat and hard work today. I know you'll all be trying your hardest, but in the end I can only pick ten. For those of you who make it, know that it will be an honour to wear the Eagles' green and gold. For those of you who don't make it, feel good that you have pushed the other players to be their best and made my decision a tough one."

Orlando shot a glance at Zack, Pete, Keegan, Cooper, Vijay, Davis, and the other players circled around the coach and knew he had his work cut out for him.

"First order of business is to get a real measure of everyone, so I want all of you to line up in a row from tallest to shortest," Coach said, extending his arms wide. "Zack, you'll be on one end for sure."

Orlando didn't think this was a very fair way to start the tryout. If the coach was just going to choose the team based on height, he should just go ahead and do it without making everyone work out. He walked slowly to the other end of the line and stood like a small period at the end of a long sentence.

Coach made every player say his name one at a time. Orlando figured that would just make it easier to know who the shortest guy was to cut.

"If you think size is how I'm going to pick the

team, you're dead wrong," Coach said. "I want the ten players who work the hardest, listen the closest, and respect their teammates the most. So take a good look around. It won't matter where you are in the line. It will only matter who rises above the others. Okay, now let's get going."

Orlando still didn't trust Coach. He thought the man was saying all the right things, but he didn't totally believe that height wasn't going to make a difference. This was basketball, after all. He just had to show Coach he had all the moves and couldn't wait to display them. He'd have to wait, though. Coach Krinski told them the first half of the tryout was going to be all conditioning without even touching a ball.

"Let's see what you guys are made of," Coach said, blowing the whistle again.

The workout started with a suicide drill that made Orlando run back and forth between gym floor lines that got farther and farther apart. By the end of the drill Orlando's legs felt like rubber and he was sucking wind badly. He wasn't alone. Some of the players were bent over gasping for breath and some were collapsed on the floor. Coach Krinski watched while taking notes on the clipboard he carried around with him at all times.

Orlando stood in line at the water fountain waiting for a drink. "Are we ever going to touch a ball?" he complained. "This blows."

Pete and Keegan were ahead of Orlando in line and turned to see who was lipping off. "We should've known it was you again."

Zack stood up from the fountain, wiped a few drops off his lips with his arm, and gave Orlando a look. "Coach just wants to make sure we can play till the final whistle. Last year we didn't have the best team in the league, but we were sure in the best shape. It helped us win a few games when the other guys ran out of gas."

In the second hour of the tryout Coach got down to basketball business. "Everyone ready to handle the ball?" he asked.

The gym was dead quiet. Almost everyone was too tired to respond.

"It's about freakin' time," Orlando said under his breath.

"Someone want to do a few more suicide drills?" Coach asked, glaring.

The players all shook their heads, narrowed their eyes and stared at Orlando.

"I know *most* of you are tired, but it's time to get your second wind," Coach said. Let's start with some layups."

I can finally show these guys what I've got, Orlando thought to himself.

"Form two lines, one for rebounding and one for driving to the basket." Coach threw a crisp pass to Zack. "Start us off, Mr. Jackson."

Zack made a few easy dribbles toward the basket, then took off from his left foot and easily laid the ball off the backboard and into the hoop with his outstretched right hand. Orlando followed him and although he couldn't reach anywhere near as high as Zack, the ball still kissed the backboard and fell softly into the net.

"That's what I'm talking about," Orlando said, giving a fist pump as he ran to the back of the rebounding line. "Piece of cake."

For the last drill Coach Krinski had the players dribble around a series of orange cones. This was one exercise where it helped being low to the ground. Orlando scooted through the course and afterwards gave a nod to the coach hoping he'd give him high marks. Orlando had been watching the rest of the players go through the drills and so far thought he was easily in the top half. He wasn't the most skilled player on the court, but he sure wasn't the worst, either. If he could keep this up he'd make the squad for sure.

Coach Krinski stood at centre court and waved in the players. "Now comes the real test," he said, scanning the twenty nervous faces gathered around him. "I'm going to break you into two groups of ten for a scrimmage. Team against team to see how you'd play in a real game. Make sure you switch up when you get tired to give the other players a chance."

Orlando had a knot in his stomach and it wasn't from tying the drawstring around his shorts too tight.

He had practiced the drills on his driveway but had never played in a five-on-five scrimmage before. Even still, he was pretty confident. He pulled a green pinny over his shirt and joined the other players on the green team. Coach Krinski put him at guard, tossed him the ball and asked him to start the game. Orlando dribbled straight up court, but the second he crossed the centre line, Pete stole the ball and raced in for an easy bucket for the red team.

The rest of the red squad cheered from the sideline. "That was too easy, Pete!"

"Protect the ball!" Coach shouted at Orlando from across the floor.

Orlando dribbled the ball up court again, but this time when Pete blocked his path he turned his back to him and held one hand out to fend him off. He dribbled backwards, backing Pete into his own half. There was no way Pete could get at the ball.

"That's better!" Coach shouted.

Orlando looked up and smiled at Coach. Big mistake. Pete came swooping in again and ripped the ball out of Orlando's hand on the way to the basket and two more points.

On his third attempt Orlando got the ball across centre and tried a quick pass to his green teammate, just on the edge of the key near the basket. It was a good hard chest pass. The only trouble was that it went straight to Zack, who was playing for the other team.

Zack grabbed the ball and with his long arms launched a football pass all the way down court to Keegan, who caught it just in front of the hoop and went straight to the rim without even a single dribble. It was already 6–0 red.

"Hey, Orlando, how about giving us a chance to screw up, too?" Cooper shouted from the green sideline.

Orlando pretended not to hear him. This wasn't the way it was supposed to go. He had to stay on and show Coach he could get the job done.

Orlando bit his lip and concentrated doubly hard as he dribbled up court again. He was careful to protect the ball and not make an early pass. He slowly backed Pete up inside his own half. Then he stopped dribbling and held the ball, looking for an open man. Orlando faked passes to the left and the right, trying to shake off Pete, who was waving his arms all over him like an octopus. Orlando had to get into a better position. He started dribbling again to make an escape.

The whistle blew right away. "Double-dribble!" Coach shouted. "Once you've stopped dribbling, you can't start again. Red ball!"

Orlando knew the rule but had never worried about it on his driveway. There, he'd stop and start dribbling any time he felt like it. He'd never had anyone draped over him trying to take the ball away, either. Playing a real game was completely different from playing at home. Orlando hung his head and walked off the court.

"Quit being a floor hog," Cooper said, running past him and finally getting a chance to play.

The red and green teams kept battling each other for another twenty minutes before Coach blew the whistle for one last time. "Okay, that's all for today. Hit the showers!"

There was a lot of shouting and joking in the locker room after the tryout. Most of the noise was by the players who thought they'd made the team. Zack, Pete, Keegan, Cooper, Vijay, and Davis were fist-bumping each other in one corner. The other corner, where Orlando sat, was dead quiet.

Orlando unlaced his shoes. His socks were sweaty and his feet were red with blisters. The tryout hadn't gone exactly as planned, but he had looked pretty good during the drills and might have earned enough points on Coach Krinski's clipboard to squeeze onto the top ten list. He figured he was right on the bubble.

Orlando wasn't sure about making the team, but he was sure about one thing. He was beat.

3 THE LIST

Orlando rolled over in bed, reached out into the darkness and stared at the time on his phone — 3:47 a.m. *Man, this is crazy!* he thought. He had tossed and turned all night, replaying every minute of the tryout and wishing he'd played better. His dream of making the Evergreen Eagles was turning into a nightmare. One that had all 720 students at Evergreen Junior High laughing at him.

No matter where he went in his nightmare they all jeered, "We know who's on the liiiissst!" They were everywhere — in the hall, in the cafeteria, even in the washroom. There was no escape. No matter how many times Orlando asked who had made it, no one would tell him. Not Zack, not Pete, not Keegan, not even Coach Krinski. All they did was taunt and point their fingers at him.

The alarm finally buzzed at seven sharp. Orlando rolled out of bed and stumbled bleary-eyed into the bathroom, hoping a hot shower would help him to wake up. Every muscle in his body ached from the try-out and he felt like he'd hardly slept. One look in the mirror and he saw the proof. His black, tightly curled hair, which he liked to comb straight up to make him look taller, was all matted down flat as a pancake. As if that wasn't bad enough, the whites of his eyes had become bloodshot. They were red as the ketchup on an order of McDonald's fries. He let the hot water stream against his face for a few extra minutes before getting out and pulling on his clothes.

Now he was behind schedule. He rushed by his dad in the kitchen, grabbed a piece of toast, and downed a glass of orange juice.

"Sleep well?" Dad asked with the same smile he gave his son every morning.

Orlando shook his head. "Worst night of my life."

"Worried about making the team?" Dad asked.

"I sucked!"

"I'm sure it wasn't that bad, here's your lunch," Dad said changing the subject and handing him a brown bag.

"Did you make this?"

"Sure did," Dad said proudly.

"Why didn't Mom?" Orlando said, still cranky.

"She's driving Megan to early-morning basketball practice before going to work.

"Figures," Orlando said, throwing the bag into his backpack.

"Mom's home as much as possible."

"Well, that's not much," Orlando said, rushing out the back door. He didn't want to miss the bus today of all days.

He sprinted down the street to the stop just as the big yellow door swung open. Most kids in Junior High didn't have a problem climbing the tall steps of the bus. But Orlando's legs were shorter than most kids' and today definitely wasn't most days. His shoe caught the edge of the top step and he crashed forward, flat on his face. He could hear the other kids laughing at him as he picked himself up and walked down the aisle to where he usually sat in the back. He liked sitting in the rear with the older kids because it made him feel bigger. One of the beefy grade-nine boys from the football team stood up and blocked his path.

"Yo dude, we're all full up."

"But I always sit back here," Orlando said.

"Not today, Shorty."

Orlando didn't have the energy to argue and slid into a seat closer to the front.

In his homeroom class Orlando slouched at his desk waiting for the day's announcements to be broadcast over the intercom. His legs felt like he'd been running suicide drills all night. He rested his head on both hands and listened. "The cafeteria menu today is meat loaf with mashed potatoes and peas," he heard the voice say. "The chess club is meeting after school, and the list of the players who made the boys' basketball team will be posted on the coach's door in the gym at lunchtime."

Orlando sat up. That was the news he was waiting for. His brain went into overdrive and for the next three hours he had a tug-of-war with himself. In language-arts class he thought he was good enough to make the team. In science he didn't think his dribbling had made the grade. In social, his last class before lunch, he re-bounded and was back to thinking he'd be picked. By lunchtime he was worn out.

The walk to the gym seemed to take forever. Orlando wondered why his legs were dragging down the hall. He felt like he had anchors attached to his feet. Maybe he was afraid of finding out. For the tryout he was the one in a rush. Today he could see Pete, Cooper, Keegan, Vijay, and Davis were already way ahead of him.

Orlando pushed through the gym doors and saw a pack of guys huddled around the coach's door. The players at the back were jumping like salmon leaping upstream. Everybody wanted a look at the sheet of white paper with ten names on it.

"This team is going to rock!" Pete said, flicking back his long black hair. He had been at the front of the pack and was now snaking his way through the crowd. He'd had the best wheels at the tryout, and Orlando knew he had a lock on making the squad.

"Did you see my name, Pete?" Orlando asked.

"No, only the good players are on the list," he said,

brushing Orlando aside. Orlando ducked under some of the taller players and pushed his way to the front. His eyes scanned down the list . . . *Zack, Pete, Keegan, Cooper, Vijay, Davis* . . . He got to number ten and still didn't see his name. "Man, I can't believe it," Orlando whispered to himself.

Orlando wasn't the only one disappointed. For every one player that made it, another one didn't. You could tell right away who were the lucky ones. They were bug-eyed with excitement, joking and pushing each other around. There were more knuckle bumps than he had ever seen. The guys who didn't make it wandered off by themselves.

"I'm sure you were number eleven," Zack called from the pack of guys who had made the team. "Maybe next year."

Yeah, all it's going to take is 365 days and about six inches in height, thought Orlando, blaming how short he was for everything. He kept his head down and shuffled out of the gym.

★★★

Orlando reached into his pocket for the key to his house. He opened the front door and threw his backpack on the floor. The bag was heavy with homework, but he didn't feel like doing any of it. Especially the math problems that Mr. Krinski had assigned. He grabbed a granola bar from the cupboard and sat at the kitchen table, waiting for his mom to come home.

She was supposed to be there. The deal was that she'd go to work early so she could come home early. But that wasn't the way it had worked. Yeah, she left early but she almost always worked late. Orlando figured that being a chemistry professor at the university must have been a busy job. His dad was an economics professor there, too. But he never made promises he couldn't keep. He didn't leave for work until after Orlando had left for school in the morning and he got home at dinnertime every night. At least Orlando knew when to expect him.

Two hours later his mom swept through the front door. "Sorry I'm late, but I have a surprise for you, Lando!" She'd call him that whenever she got excited.

Orlando looked up from the couch where he had been watching TV. He saw that his mom was holding a round object about the size of a basketball all wrapped up in green paper.

"Gee, I wonder what it is?" he said, rolling his eyes.

"We thought you'd like a new ball," she said, smiling. "So I stopped off at a sports store and picked up the official NBA model. "It's to celebrate your making the team."

"You have to make the team before you can celebrate," Orlando said, shaking his head. Didn't she know anything?

His mom gently put the ball down on the table.

"I'm sure you'll make it next time."

"There's not going to be a next time," he shot back. "I'm just too short."

"What about those players we looked up on the Internet who played for NBA teams even though they weren't tall?" his mom asked. "Earl Boykins was only five-foot-five and he made it. Muggsy Bogues was the shortest at only five-three and he played for fourteen years."

Orlando turned to walk away. "Yeah, but they were still both taller than me."

It didn't seem like anything his mom could say was going to change Orlando's mind.

For the next few hours Orlando moped around. He knew he was feeling sorry for himself, but he just couldn't help it. After dinner he went outside and shot a few baskets with his old scuffed-up ball. He didn't know where his mom had put the new ball and he didn't care. He packed his practice in early and headed straight to his room, forgetting about the cup of hot chocolate his mom usually made him before bed. There was only one thing that could cheer him up after a day like today.

Orlando plugged in.

"Welcome to HOOP Radio — the favourite station of the basketball nation. We're in Beantown for tonight's game between the Toronto Raptors and the Boston Celtics. It's going to be quite a battle with the Raps trying to rebound after

a blow-out loss against the Bulls two nights ago. It's not easy coming back after a big setback, but sometimes you just have to suck it up and get back out on the court and give it your best. If you keep working hard, good things will happen."

Todd and Ted had no idea what they were talking about, Orlando thought. Sometimes you're just too short to play.

Most nights, Orlando would listen to the first quarter of the game before falling asleep. But not tonight. Yawning, he hit the power button, slid the computer onto the bedside table, and closed his eyes. He was asleep in seconds.

4 LUCKY BREAK

Mr. Krinski stood by the blackboard at the front of the class. He wore a navy blue sweater over khaki pants and brown loafers. He adjusted the glasses that sat on his long pointy nose and looked around the class. "Let's go over the homework I assigned for last night."

Orlando gulped. He hadn't done his math homework. He'd been too busy feeling sorry for himself and being mad at Mr. Krinski for not picking him. All he had wanted to do was forget about the list and listen to the game on HOOP Radio.

Orlando ducked, hoping Mr. Krinski wouldn't see him at his desk. He sat at the back, which was a new spot for him. All through elementary school the teachers made him sit in the front row. Now that he was in junior high he sat where he wanted, and that was at the back. For the first time he hoped being short might help to make him invisible. He leaned forward, his chest on the desk.

"Mr. O'Malley," Mr. Krinski said, "can you tell me what the square root of twenty-five is?"

Orlando's heart jumped. "I'm . . . not . . . sure."

"It was part of your homework."

"I didn't have time to finish all the questions."

"It was the very first question," Mr. Krinski said, glaring.

By now the whole class was staring at Orlando. But no one was laughing because they all knew Mr. K might call on them next. The teacher left Orlando alone and moved on to other students to answer the rest of the questions. Finally the bell rang. Orlando packed up his books and headed for the door.

"Mr. O'Malley, I'd like to see you," Mr. Krinski said sternly, sitting behind his desk.

Orlando stood in front of him expecting the worst. He'd probably get a detention. "You know it's important to do your homework, right?"

"Right."

"And it won't happen again, right?"

"Right."

Orlando turned and started walking toward the door.

"There's one more thing," Mr. Krinski said.

Here comes the bad news, Orlando thought.

"You're on the basketball team. Davis broke his arm skateboarding last night and won't be able to play for most of the season. You were my next pick from the tryout. So, congratulations, and I hope you're ready to play. Our first game is after school today."

Orlando stood frozen like a statue. He heard Mr. Krinski, but he couldn't quite believe the words he was saying.

"Don't you have another class right now?"

"Yes, sir."

"Then you better get moving."

Orlando snapped out of his trance, turned and marched out. He'd never left math class with a grin this big before.

★★★

Coach Krinski stood in the middle of the locker room holding a big box of uniforms. "Every time you put on these green and gold colours I want you to think about making your school proud. The Evergreen Eagles have a long history of great basketball teams and I know you guys will follow the tradition. Come on over and select your number. Zack, as the captain this year, you get to choose first."

Nine players lined up behind the tall blond centre. Orlando stood at the rear and sized up the starting five. He already knew Zack was the tallest player on the team and probably a league all-star. Pete was blazing fast and his long, straight black hair flicked back and forth every time he ran up court. Keegan had curly brown hair and could jump like a kangaroo. His legs were like coiled springs that made grabbing rebounds look easy. Cooper had a shock of thick copper hair and was sneaky quick. He could steal the ball from a bank vault. Vijay had dark hair and wide-set dark eyes that helped him see the whole court at once. He could pass like Canadian basketball legend Steve Nash and find an open man with his eyes closed.

Pete, Keegan, Cooper, Vijay, and the rest of the team picked their shirts before Orlando got his turn. He rummaged through the box until he found what he was looking for — number 00.

"What's with the two zeroes?" Zack asked.

Orlando grinned. "They're letters, as in O O for Orlando O'Malley."

"Welcome to the team, Double-O," Zack said. "Davis was a good player and you've got some big shoes to fill until he's back."

Not every one agreed with the coach's decision to put Orlando on the squad. He overheard the starting guards whisper a few comments questioning his ability.

"We've got to play the whole regular season with this guy?" Vijay said, tying his shoes in the corner.

"He seems kind of small," Pete said.

"Except when it comes to his mouth," Keegan said.

"How's he ever going to get a shot away?" Cooper asked, shaking his head.

"Did you see his uniform?" Vijay added. "It was like ten sizes too big."

Orlando looked down at his shorts. Sure enough they hung below his knees. They were almost like pants. His shirt didn't fit much better. The green-and-gold uniform made him look even smaller, but he was proud to wear it just the same. It was the first real team he had ever played for.

Out in the gym Coach Krinski stood in front of the Eagles bench like a general addressing his troops. "The Hilldale Hawks are a good team. Last year they went all the way to city finals and won the championship. We're going to have to work hard and play smart. Starting five get ready. Now, everyone together on three."

Orlando wedged himself between the other players and reached into the middle of the pack with his hand. "One . . . two . . . three . . . Eagles!"

The circle broke with five players trotting out onto the floor while Orlando and four others sat on the bench. Zack won the opening tip from the referee at centre court and flicked the ball back to Keegan, who dribbled into Hawks territory. The Eagles whipped the ball around the three-point line from Pete to Cooper to Vijay and back to Keegan, who bounced it inside to Zack under the basket.

"Here comes two points!" Orlando yelled from the bench. "No one can stop Zack from inside!"

But the players wearing the red uniforms weren't listening. Just as Zack went up to lay the ball in off the backboard, a long arm skied even higher than Zack's and swatted it away to the corner, where a Hawks teammate scooped it up and threw it down court for a fast break. The Hawks speedy forward caught the ball over his shoulder and in one smooth motion laid the ball into the Eagles basket. The referee held up two fingers and the scoreboard showed the first points of the game.

Orlando could see why the Hawks were ranked number one in the city. The game was fast-paced with players running full tilt up and down the court. The only problem was that for every one basket the Eagles made, the Hawks made two. Coach Krinski looked at the 24–12 score and called a time-out.

"We've got to slow down their fast break, guys. Orlando, go in for Keegan."

Keegan, out of breath, walked toward Orlando. "Watch number 22," he gasped on his way to the bench. "He's like a rocket."

Orlando took the inbounds pass from Pete and dribbled into the Hawks court, making sure he protected the ball. Out of the corner of his eye he spotted Vijay on the wing. It would be a risky throw all the way across court, but Vijay looked wide open. If he could make the pass he'd show Coach what a good playmaker he was. Orlando fired the ball over the heads of two Hawks but not the third. Before the ball could get to Vijay a red flash with number 22 on his back intercepted the pass and dribbled all the way up court before pulling up at the top of thc Eaglcs kcy and hitting a jumper.

"I told you to watch 22!" Keegan shouted from the bench.

Orlando glanced up at the scoreboard and saw there were only thirty seconds left in the first half. He was determined to make up for his mistake. He drove the ball up court, looking for Zack in the middle. He hit the big centre with a perfect bounce pass and ran to the open corner, where Zack returned the favour by passing him the ball with just three clicks left on the clock. Orlando thought he could sink the shot even though a Hawks defender had his arms up right in front of his face. He launched the ball extra high over the Hawks player and it came up way short of the basket and just grazing the bottom of the net. "Air ball!" yelled one of the Hawks.

It was a bad shot and Orlando knew it. The buzzer sounded to end the half with the Hawks up 44–32.

The teams had a ten-minute break at halftime. Coach Krinski talked to the players while they drank from their water bottles. Orlando stood a few steps away from the group, knowing he had screwed up, but close enough that he could still hear every word. Coach tried to pump up the Eagles by saying the game wasn't over yet. But no one was buying it. These were the Hawks, after all, practically unbeatable.

"We aren't good enough to beat the Hawks," Keegan said woefully.

"Especially with guys like Double-O on our team," Pete added.

"More like Double Zero," Vijay said. "Did you see that lame shot?"

Zack glared at his teammates. "That's enough! We're all in this together. We win as a team and we lose as a team. Everyone is playing the best he can."

Orlando was surprised their best player was taking his side. Still, he figured Coach would pull him from the game and went to sit alone on the end of the bench. *Maybe I'm not good enough to play for the Eagles,* he thought. He wasn't helping the team, he was hurting it.

The second half started pretty much like the first one ended. The Hawks kept bringing it and built a commanding 16-point lead. The Eagles bench was silent. Not even Coach Krinski was saying much.

If Orlando couldn't help the team on the court, maybe he could help them sitting right here on the bench. He remembered what Todd and Ted had said on HOOP Radio about not giving up and good things will happen. He wondered how they would call this game if they were doing the play-by-play. Orlando knew there was only one way to find out. He put on his deepest, most booming voice and started announcing from the far end of the bench.

"THINGS AREN'T LOOKING GOOD OUT THERE FOR THE EVERGREEN EAGLES THIS AFTERNOON, FOLKS. THEIR WINGS HAVE BEEN CLIPPED BUT THEY'VE GOT TO REMEMBER IT'S NEVER OVER TILL IT'S OVER. HERE COMES KEEGAN BRINGING THE BALL UP COURT. HE PASSES IT OVER TO COOPER, WHO RELAYS IT OVER TO ZACK IN THE KEY, WHO HITS THE HOOK SHOT FOR TWO.

THE HAWKS BRING THE BALL UP AND OVER THE CENTRE LINE, BUT IT'S STOLEN BY PETE, WHO SLASHES HIS WAY TO THE BASKET AND LAYS IT IN FOR TWO MORE! NOW WE'VE GOT OURSELVES A BALL GAME!"

All the Eagle players on the bench turned to watch Orlando. Whatever he was doing was working. The Eagles were playing better: diving for loose balls, rebounding in the paint, hitting the open man. Every time Orlando announced another basket for the Eagles, one or two of his teammates would stand and cheer.

"THIS UNDERDOG GROUP OF KIDS FROM EVERGREEN JUNIOR HIGH IS CLAWING THEIR WAY BACK INTO THE GAME. DOWN BY AS MANY AS 16, THE EAGLES HAVE CUT THE HAWKS' LEAD TO JUST THREE POINTS. FASTEN YOUR SEAT BELTS EVERYONE. THIS GAME IS GOING DOWN TO THE WIRE!"

Now the entire Eagles bench was on its feet. Orlando could see Coach Krinski asking himself whether he should tell him to cool it, but how could he? The Eagles were on a roll, and so was Orlando.

"IT'S ALL COMING DOWN TO THE FINAL MINUTE. THE HAWKS LOOK RATTLED, AND WHY SHOULDN'T THEY? NO ONE SAW THIS FREIGHT TRAIN COMING. THE HAWKS THROW IT IN, BUT THE PASS IS INTERCEPTED BY A DIVING COOPER, WHO TOSSES IT TO KEEGAN BEFORE HE EVEN HITS THE FLOOR. WHAT A PLAY! KEEGAN RUNS A GIVE-AND-GO WITH ZACK. HE TAKES THE RETURN PASS AND HITS THE REVERSE LAYUP FROM UNDER THE

BASKET, SLICING THE LEAD TO JUST ONE. THE CLOCK IS IN THE FINAL TWENTY SECONDS. HOLD ON TO YOUR HATS!"

The action on the court was furious. Not wanting to miss a single play, Orlando and the Eagles stood on the bench to get a better view. Sitting or standing, Orlando continued to call the game.

"NUMBER 22 IS BRINGING THE BALL UP FOR THE HAWKS. WE KNOW HE'S FAST, BUT HE'S NO MATCH FOR THE SPEED OF PETE 'THE HUMAN FLASH' WHO APPEARS OUT OF NOWHERE TO STEAL THE ROCK. HE'S GOT A BREAK. THERE'S NOTHING BETWEEN HIM AND THE NET. HE LAUNCHES FROM THE KEY AND PUTS UP THE SHOT. THIS IS FOR THE WIN! THE BALL ROLLS AROUND AND AROUND THE RIM BEFORE . . . IT SPINS OUT. OHHH, THAT WAS SO CLOSE! THE FINAL BUZZER SOUNDS AND THE HAWKS HOLD ON TO ESCAPE WITH A WIN. BUT WHAT A GRITTY EFFORT FROM THAT EAGLES SQUAD. THEY'RE GOING TO BE A TEAM TO WATCH THIS YEAR!"

In the locker room after the game Coach Krinski talked to the players. "That was a great comeback. Every one of you should be proud. Even the guys on the bench played a big role, especially our star announcer." He looked at Orlando.

Zack came over and slapped Orlando five. "Nice work, Double-O. We could hear you on the court and you kept us going. I think you freaked the Hawks out a bit, too."

"We couldn't have made it close without you," Cooper said.

"I was wrong before," Pete agreed.

Keegan nodded. "We need you on the team, man."

Orlando was still only five-foot-two, but standing in the locker room after the game he felt a little taller.

5 SERIOUSLY

Orlando slept like a log. Now that he was on the team, the nightmare of the previous evening didn't return and he bounced out of bed ready for his morning shower. He shoved his feet into his slippers and scooted out of his bedroom. Down the hall he saw the bathroom door was closed, which could only mean one thing — Megan was still in there. He stood by the door and spoke loudly enough for anyone inside to hear him.

"I'M HERE REPORTING TO YOU LIVE FROM OUTSIDE THE O'MALLEY BATHROOM, WHERE A FOURTEEN-YEAR-OLD GIRL NAMED MEGAN HAS LOCKED HERSELF INSIDE IN A FUTILE ATTEMPT TO MAKE HERSELF LOOK GOOD. OH SURE, SHE CAN PUT ON MAKEUP, BUT IN THE END SHE'S STILL GOING TO LOOK PRETTY . . . AS IN PRETTY PLAIN. SO IF YOU CAN HEAR ME IN THERE, WHY DON'T YOU JUST GIVE UP AND COME OUT SO YOUR BETTER-LOOKING BROTHER CAN GET READY FOR SCHOOL?"

"Leave your sister alone and come have your breakfast first," his mom called from downstairs.

Orlando walked into the kitchen, followed just seconds later by the sound of footsteps charging down the stairs. Megan's long blond hair was perfectly brushed and her lips looked pink and glossy. She wore tight blue jeans, a white buttoned shirt, and was in a hurry as usual.

"I heard you made the team," she said.

"Nothing to it," Orlando said, not wanting to let on he hadn't made it at first.

"I should come and check you guys out sometime. See if you're anywhere near as good as our squad at Maplewood. We rock and we're going all the way this year."

"Maybe sometime," Orlando said, hoping she didn't come by to watch before he started to play better. Plus, he still wasn't sure how Pete, Keegan, Cooper, and Vijay really felt about him. He did say some pretty dumb things to them before the tryout.

Megan tapped her fingers impatiently on the kitchen table. "Mom, are we ready to leave yet or what? I've got a practice to get to, you know."

"Just a minute, Megs," Mom said, putting a brown bag on the counter in front of Orlando. "I made you lunch this morning."

"Good, because Dad didn't even put butter on the bread yesterday," Orlando said, shaking his head and rolling his eyes. "What was he thinking?"

★★★

For the next couple of weeks the Eagles had practices scheduled for almost every day after school. It was the beginning of the season and they had a lot of plays to learn. Orlando thought their first practice after their first game was pretty much like the tryout. In other words, exhausting.

First, there was a series of shooting and conditioning exercises that ended with the infamous suicide drill. Orlando thought that running up and down between the lines might get easier each time he did it, but it sure didn't feel that way. He still sucked wind and grabbed his water bottle as soon as he could afterwards. The only good news was that he wasn't the only one. Zack and the rest of the guys still suffered as well.

Orlando was stoked for the drills to end and the scrimmage to start. Since Coach made all the cuts, the team was now down to ten players, so there wouldn't be any substitutions. Everybody would get to play all the time. The game went up and down the court with Orlando's green team hitting a few more buckets than the red squad. Orlando was surprised to be leading because Zack was on the red team. The big guy was usually on the winning squad, but today he seemed distracted and was just loafing out there. That wasn't like Zack.

A few minutes before the end of the scrimmage, a tall blond girl wearing blue jeans and a white shirt walked into the gym. She climbed into the stands and sat down to watch the game. The seats were empty except for her.

Orlando saw that Zack couldn't seem to take his eyes off the girl. Suddenly, however, he was a new player. He went high to grab rebounds at his end of the court and was a one-man scoring machine at the other end. Every time he got his big hands on the ball near the key, he drove to the basket and put two points up on the board. He was unstoppable.

Orlando couldn't resist putting on his announcer's hat. "WHAT HAS GOT INTO ZACK JACKSON? A MINUTE AGO HE WAS JUST A WASHED-UP JUNIOR-HIGH PLAYER AND NOW HE'S PLAYING LIKE AN NBA ALL-STAR! YOU SAW IT WITH YOUR OWN EYES, FANS."

Keegan and Cooper burst out laughing so hard they could barely keep playing. Luckily, Coach Krinski blew the whistle to end the scrimmage and the boys trotted into the locker room.

"You were on fire there at the end, Zack," Keegan said as their tired bodies slumped on the bench. Zack just smiled a sheepish grin.

"It was like you turned into LeBron or something," Cooper joked.

"Must be his shoes." Vijay laughed, pointing at Zack's size-twelve Nike LeBron kicks.

"Not even Orlando could stop you," Pete mocked while flicking back his long black hair.

Even Orlando found this funny, knowing there was no way he could ever stop Zack.

After they were dressed, Orlando overheard Zack talking to Pete. "I don't know who she is. But I'm going to find out."

Zack went one by one down the line of players asking who the girl was in the stands. No one seemed to know.

"Why don't you ask me?" Orlando asked.

"You're new at Evergreen," Zack said. "I doubt you'd know who she was. Besides she's way out of your league."

"Try me."

Now the whole team was paying attention.

Zack grinned. "Okay, smart guy, who's the tall blond girl?"

"Isn't it obvious? She's my sister."

"Yeah, that's a good one!" Cooper hooted.

"Where do you come up with this stuff?" Keegan kidded. "First doing the play-by-play of the game and now this. Man, you are one funny dude."

"Seriously, she's my sister. Her name is Megan. She's fourteen, just like me."

Zack studied Orlando's face. "You're serious, aren't you."

"I'm telling you, man, she's my sister."

"How can you both be the same age and in the same family and not look anything alike?" Zack asked, screwing his face up like a twisted locker-room towel.

Orlando sighed heavily. He had to tell his story for the millionth time. "I was adopted as a baby from Haiti. My mom and dad already had a kid and that was Megan. They wanted a boy."

"So that girl who was in the stands really is your sister," Zack said, starting to believe the story.

Orlando nodded. "She's probably waiting for me outside," he said.

"So how come I've never seen her around before?" Zack asked.

"I was tired of people asking so many questions when we both went to the same place. Just like you're asking. So now she goes to one school and I go to another."

Orlando and the rest of the team left the locker room and walked into the gym. Sure enough, the blond girl was standing there waiting with her arms crossed.

"What took you so long?" Megan asked Orlando. "Mom wants us home early so they can go out to dinner. She's in the car waiting. I haven't got all day."

Zack elbowed Orlando in the shoulder while smiling straight at Megan. "Oh yeah, and this is my friend Zack."

"Yeah, whatever," Megan said, turning to leave and not even looking at Zack. "Let's go."

6 LAST LETTER IN H-O-R-S-E

Orlando's head buzzed. He cracked open his eyes and saw his phone vibrating on the table beside his bed.

"Hello," he said groggily.

"Orlando, wake up. It's Zack."

"What are you calling me so early on Saturday for?" Orlando said still half-asleep.

"It's already eleven o'clock, dude," Zack said.

"I need my sleep, man. I'm still growing." Orlando chuckled.

"I was thinking we should shoot baskets together sometime," Zack said.

"What are you talking about?" Orlando said. "We shoot baskets almost every day at school."

"True, but we don't shoot them at other places," Zack said. "Sometimes it's good to test out other courts so you can feel confident playing anywhere."

"So, where were you thinking of playing?" Orlando asked.

"I don't know, somebody's house maybe," Zack said.

"You have a basket. Why don't we go to your house?" Orlando suggested.

"Naw, the mesh is pretty old and needs replacing," Zack said as if he had already made up an excuse.

Orlando was wide awake now. "Why don't you come over to my house?" This was great. It wasn't every day he could invite over the star of the basketball team.

"Hey, good idea!" Zack said. "I'm glad you thought of it."

"When do you want to shoot?" Orlando asked, thinking it might be tomorrow or at the very earliest later that afternoon.

"How about right now?" Zack suggested.

"I guess," Orlando said. "Give me an hour. I've got to eat some breakfast."

"You mean lunch." Zack laughed.

Orlando hung up, glad the best athlete at school wanted to be his friend but still wondering what was the big rush.

★★★

"Why don't we play HORSE?" Orlando suggested. He and Zack had just been shooting around and now it was time for some friendly competition. It was a sunny October afternoon, perfect weather for Orlando to show his tall friend just who ruled O'Malley court.

"You're on," Zack said. "Show me your best shot."

Orlando took the pass from Zack and started dribbling toward the basket like he was going to do another ordinary layup. Then as he took off, he whipped the ball behind his back and laid it up off the backboard.

Zack watched the ball fall through the hoop. "Nice around-the-back layup."

"Nothing to it." Orlando grinned.

Now it was Zack's turn. He took the ball and tried to copy exactly what Orlando had done. He started dribbling toward the basket, but when the ball was half-way behind his back he lost control and it flew off onto the grass beside the driveway.

"What a tough break," Orlando kidded. "You've got an 'H.'"

The boys continued the game showing off their best moves. Orlando hit three-point jumpers from out-side and Zack countered with hook shots from the low post. The game was tied H-O-R-S to H-O-R-S when Megan came jogging out of the garage, her blond hair bouncing behind her in a ponytail. She wore baggy grey sweatpants and an old white T-shirt with the words Ontario Junior All-Stars on it.

"Mind if I play?" Megan demanded more than asked.

Oh great, thought Orlando. *That's all we need. My stupid sister playing with us.*

"We're pretty busy here, Megs. We don't have time to play with girls, right, Zack?"

Zack smiled. "It's okay with me if Megan wants to play."

"Are you sure?" Orlando said, looking Zack square in the eye. "She's a girl, you know."

Zack turned to Megan and showed off by holding the ball in just his big left hand. "Let me explain how the game HORSE is played. First —"

"I'm familiar with the rules, Stretch," Megan interrupted. "Let's play."

Zack flipped the ball to Megan. "Next one to get the letter 'E' loses," he challenged.

Orlando wasn't crazy about his sister cutting in on their game. *Zack only came over to play with me, right?* Then again, he didn't think Zack knew what he was in for, either. He thought this was too good an opportunity not to announce.

"THE H-O-R-S-E SHOWDOWN HAS COME TO THE FINISH LINE. DOES THE NEW GIRL HAVE ANY CHANCE OF WINNING? WE DON'T THINK SO BUT WE'RE ABOUT TO FIND OUT. MEGAN O'MALLEY GRABS THE BALL AND TAKES IT TO THE END OF THE DRIVEWAY. SHE CUTS AROUND ORLANDO, HER SHORTER BUT FAR MORE TALENTED BROTHER, DRIBBLING THE BALL BETWEEN HER LEGS AS SHE GOES. NOW SHE'S BOUNCING THE BALL BEHIND HER BACK SLASHING AROUND ZACK LIKE HE'S AN ORANGE PYLON AND NOT THE STAR OF THE EVERGREEN EAGLES. MEGAN LEAVES ZACK IN HER DUST AND IS NOW IN FULL STRIDE, DRIVING

STRAIGHT IN FRONT OF THE HOOP WHERE SHE PUTS UP THE SHOT . . ."

Orlando could see Megan had thrown the ball too hard. "Nice try, sis."

"So close," Zack said. He sounded relieved the ball was about to bounce hard off the backboard.

Orlando took one look at Megan's intense blue eyes and realized his sister wasn't finished her shot.

"WAIT A MINUTE, SPORTS FANS! MEGAN IS STILL GOING. THE BLOND O'MALLEY FLEXES HER LONG LEGS AND LAUNCHES HERSELF UP TOWARD THE RIM, WHERE SHE CATCHES THE BALL COMING OFF THE BACKBOARD AND LAYS IT BACK UP INTO THE BASKET WITH HER RIGHT HAND. SHE MISSED THE SHOT ON PURPOSE AND SINKS THE REBOUND ALL WHILE HANGING IN MIDAIR!"

Orlando watched the ball fall softly through the mesh and land in Megan's waiting hands. She flipped it to Zack.

"Let's see you make that, big guy."

Orlando knew he couldn't make a trick shot like that in a million years and was pretty sure not even Zack could.

"I'll just take the 'E,'" Zack said, apparently not wanting to embarrass himself trying to make the circus shot he'd just seen.

"You're darn right you'll take it," Megan said. "And where I go to school that spells HORSE."

"Where do you go to school?" Zack said with surprising interest.

"Maplewood."

"And do you happen to play hoops at Maplewood?" Zack asked.

"Captain of the girls' team," Megan said, not bragging.

Zack smiled and shook his head. "That explains a lot."

"Well, I've got to bounce," Megan said.

"Yeah, see you later," Orlando said happy to see his sister leave. He was starting to wonder who Zack really wanted to shoot hoops with.

"Are you sure?" Zack asked, sounding disappointed. "You just got here."

"Going to a movie with some friends," Megan said.

"Boyfriends?" Zack asked.

"Girlfriends," Megan said.

"Do you ever go to other shows?" Zack asked.

"Like what?" Megan asked.

"Like the show we'll put on at our next basketball game," Zack said.

Orlando wasn't convinced that watching the Evergreen Junior High Eagles was quite the same as going to a Batman or Spiderman blockbuster. Zack was good but he was no superhero.

Megan stared at Zack. "I just got a preview of that show and I'm not sure I found it that entertaining," Megan said. "I don't know if I'd get my money's worth."

"But you'll think about it, right?" Zack asked. "You don't need a ticket or anything."

Megan was halfway to the garage when she called over her shoulder, "Maybe."

Zack and Orlando shot a few more hoops as the sun got lower in the western sky.

"Did you know Megan played basketball?" Zack asked Orlando.

"She's my sister, dude. What do you think?"

7 THE SUBSTITUTE

Orlando sat slumped in the school cafeteria. He was worried.

"Is the lunch special that bad?" Zack kidded, plunking himself down beside him and stretching his long legs under the table. He studied the sliced turkey, green peas, and mashed mystery food that lay on Orlando's plate and shook his head. "Good thing that's covered with gravy."

"How about you try a bite before I do?"

"Not even *I'm* that hungry." Zack grinned.

"Are you sure? Maybe pretend I'm the king and you're the royal food taster, making sure I'm not being poisoned by my enemies."

"Me thinks King Orlando has to eat his own lunch," Zack said, bowing like a servant from the Middle Ages.

Orlando sighed. His mom had had to leave extra early for work this morning and hadn't had time to make him a sandwich. His dad had been going to make lunch, but after the last time decided not to and gave him a few dollars instead. He made Orlando promise not to buy what he really wanted — a hot dog and fries. Orlando looked down at his plate covered in brown goop and thought, *This is what I get for doing what I'm told.*

The other Eagles slid in to the long cafeteria table.

"Someone better call 9-1-1, because we've got a lunch emergency," Pete said, holding up his thumb and little finger to his ear pretending to make a call.

"You're looking a little green, Double-O," Keegan said. "And I don't think it's the peas."

"The food's not making me feel sick, but the math quiz I have after lunch sure is," Orlando said. He picked over the turkey, finally giving up and putting down his fork. "I couldn't eat even if I wanted to."

"Did you study?" Zack asked.

Orlando nodded.

"Did you pass the last quiz?" Pete asked.

Orlando nodded.

"And was the meal you just ate fifty percent delicious and fifty percent nutritious?" Cooper joked.

Orlando played along and nodded again.

"Then you're a hundred percent ready," Vijay said as everyone groaned.

"That math joke was a real turkey!" Keegan said, getting in one final dig.

Orlando had to admit that when it came to his test he was probably making a mountain out of molehill.

He just hoped he wasn't asked to calculate the height of the mountain.

Thirty minutes later, Orlando took a deep breath and stepped into room 201. He kept his head down and trudged straight down the aisle to his regular desk at the back. He got out his freshly sharpened pencils, then looked up expecting to see Mr. Krinski standing at the front of the class holding an armful of test papers. But tall Mr. K with the moustache was nowhere in sight. Instead a small, grey-haired woman wearing a mousy brown dress stood by the desk. She looked nervous.

The woman gave a small cough in an apparent effort to clear her throat. "Class . . . class," she said, trying to be heard over the chatter of twenty-three kids who kept talking among themselves. "My name is Mrs. Appleby and I'll be your substitute teacher today. Mr. Krinski is off sick."

Suddenly all the talking and laughing came to an immediate halt. Orlando and the other students in the room stopped what they were doing as soon as they heard the magic word: *substitute*. They could sense the temporary teacher was weak and now they were like a pack of wolves moving in for the kill.

"So there's no quiz today?" a girl in the front row asked excitedly.

"No, there'll be no quiz," Mrs. Appleby said.

The class exploded in cheers and went right back to talking as if the teacher wasn't even there. Orlando knew he should take pity on Mrs. Appleby. He could see she was just as nervous about teaching the class as he had been about taking the quiz. But he was so happy the test was cancelled he couldn't control himself. He had a built-in audience and launched into play-by-play mode.

"WE'RE COMING TO YOU LIVE FROM ROOM 201 ON THE SECOND FLOOR OF EVERGREEN JUNIOR HIGH, WHERE A MAJOR ANNOUNCEMENT HAS JUST BEEN MADE. THERE WILL BE NO MATH QUIZ TODAY!"

Every head in the class turned toward the back. They had never heard Orlando announce before. He wondered how they'd react to the small guy with the big voice. The guy no one ever noticed. He stopped worrying after everyone broke out laughing. For the first time in his life he had the attention of his classmates. He wasn't being picked on. He wasn't being ignored. He wasn't being laughed at. He was the centre of the action, and he liked it. Orlando knew he had them hanging on every word.

"THE OVERMATCHED TEACHER IS TRYING TO SAY SOMETHING, BUT THE CLASS IS MAKING TOO MUCH NOISE. YOU MIGHT EXPECT TO HEAR THIS MUCH RACKET AT A RAPTORS GAME IN THE AIR CANADA CENTRE, BUT IN A MATH CLASSROOM? YOU'VE GOT TO BE KIDDING ME. THIS CROWD'S GOING WILD!"

Mrs. Appleby's face flushed with frustration as she put her hands on her hips. She turned her back on the class and wrote *QUIET!* on the blackboard. She pressed so hard the chalk snapped in two. As Orlando expected, this had the opposite effect on the kids. The decibel level of the noise just ratcheted up. It was now a small-scale riot.

"NOW THE CROWD IS ON ITS FEET. SOME MEMBERS OF THE CLASS ARE VISITING WITH THEIR FRIENDS AT OTHER DESKS. SOME HAVE GONE TO THE WASHROOM. AND SOME HAVE EVEN GONE ALL THE WAY TO THE CAFETERIA. WILL THEY COME BACK FOR THE SECOND HALF TO LEARN SOME MATH? THIS REPORTER HAS HIS DOUBTS."

Mrs. Appleby finally snapped as well. She picked up her purse from the desk and stomped out the door, shaking her bony finger at the class as she went. Orlando could tell she was saying something because her lips were moving, but there was such a racket going on he couldn't hear a single word. That was probably a good thing since most likely the teacher's comment wasn't a polite one about how well the class was behaved. The kids started to sing the song you hear at the end of NHL hockey games when their team is about the win. "*Sha-na-na-na . . . a-na-na-na . . . Hey, hey, hey . . . Goodbye!*"

"THERE YOU HAVE IT, MATH FANS. THIS AFTER-NOON'S GAME WAS A SHUTOUT WITH THE FINAL SCORE, THE CLASS ONE AND MRS. APPLEBY THE SUBSTITUTE TEACHER ZERO."

8 THE COURTROOM

Orlando sat in a hard wooden chair outside the principal's office anxiously waiting for his mom to arrive. Mrs. Pollock, the school principal, had called her at home that morning, Orlando knew, to ask her to attend a meeting in her office at 10:00 a.m. His dad had also been invited, but he was away at an economics conference in Ottawa. That was lucky. He couldn't imagine having both his parents show up at school.

At breakfast, Orlando's mom had asked him what it was all about. He'd furrowed his brow, shrugged his shoulders, and said he had no idea. He wasn't a very good liar. His mom wasn't very happy about having to leave her job at the university for a couple of hours, either. She said she was in the middle of an important chemistry experiment in the laboratory and had to put it on hold.

At 9:59 a.m. she came rushing around the corner and sat down beside him. Orlando checked the clock, then held his fist in front of his mouth like a microphone.

"IT WAS CLOSE BUT SHE MADE IT. ARRIVING JUST MOMENTS BEFORE THE TRIAL OF THE CENTURY IS MRS. O'MALLEY, MOTHER OF THE WRONGFULLY ACCUSED. IN THIS COURT, JUST LIKE ON THE BASKETBALL COURT, HE WILL SOON BE FOUND INNOCENT OF ALL FOULS."

"Shh!" Orlando's mom said. "This isn't the time or the place."

A minute later Mr. Krinski showed up and he wasn't alone. Mrs. Appleby was with him! Orlando stopped thinking about announcing and slumped in his chair. Things were going from bad to worse.

The principal's secretary popped her head out of the office door like a mouse looking out its hole. "You can all go in now."

Principal Pollock sat like a judge behind a big oak desk. There were four empty chairs in front of her. Instead of a black robe she wore a black sweater. She had a smile on her face, but Orlando knew that could change to a scowl in a flash. He'd heard she had a quick temper.

"Thank you for coming," she said, brushing back her grey hair and putting on her glasses. "Make yourselves comfortable."

Mr. Krinski, Mrs. Appleby, Orlando, and his mom all sat down. But Orlando was anything but comfortable. He felt like he was in the witness box in a courtroom waiting for the questioning to start. He didn't have to wait long.

Principal Pollock slowly turned her face from person to person as she spoke. "It has come to my attention that we had a situation in a classroom yesterday that was uncalled for. I've invited you all here so that we can get to the bottom of it."

Suddenly all eyes were on Orlando. He could see his mom was upset. *She must be wondering why everyone is staring at me.* Orlando had butterflies in his stomach again.

"Mrs. Appleby, maybe you'd like to start us off," the principal said.

"Well," she began quietly, "I was doing my very best to fill in for Mr. Krinski, who was sick."

"And still is." Mr. Krinski sniffled.

"He had assured me that they were a well-behaved group of children and that I had nothing to worry about."

"And was that the case?" Principal Pollock asked.

"Nothing could be further from the truth," Mrs. Appleby said, her voice rising.

Orlando's mom jumped in. "I teach at the university and there's always a little bit of noise at the beginning of a class while the students get settled."

"A little bit of noise?" Mrs. Appleby said, her eyes popping wide open. "It was like a wild rock-and-roll concert."

"I'm sure you're exaggerating," Mr. Krinski said, then sneezed.

"It was out of control right from the opening bell," Mrs. Appleby went on. "There was shouting, laughing, and general horsing around. Music from iPods and phones was being played at high volume. Katy Perry has no place in my classroom. No one would sit down at his or her desk to pay attention. I think even a food fight broke out at one point. It was mayhem. There was total disregard for any authority whatsoever. And all the kids were being egged on by a small boy at the back of the class who was reporting the proceedings like he was some kind of radio announcer at a sports event."

"And is that boy in this room today?" Principal Pollock asked.

"Yes, the little troublemaker is sitting right there." Mrs. Appleby pointed at Orlando.

"That doesn't sound like Orlando," his mom said, knowing that he wasn't a troublemaker at home. "I'm sure if you had asked my son to stop, he would have."

"I asked several times, but he kept right on going, just like that pink bunny on TV. I think he even enjoyed it."

Principal Pollock's eyes narrowed as she looked at Orlando. "Is all this true?"

"Everything except the Katy Perry part," Orlando said with a small grin. "I think it was actually Shakira."

"This isn't the time for jokes," his mom said, no doubt shocked that her boy was the ringleader. "Why would you do this, Orlando?"

Orlando thought for a moment, then answered honestly, "I guess I liked all the attention."

"Don't you get enough attention at home?"

"I guess, but it's not the same," Orlando said, turning to his mom. "You guys *have* to listen to me, you're my parents. "At school I'm just the little guy no one ever notices. When I called the play-by-play in math class, everyone laughed. I thought if they liked me a bit with a little announcing, they'd like me a lot if I announced even more." Orlando realized he had stepped over the line and owed Mrs. Appleby an apology.

"I have a theory," Mr. Krinski said through his stuffed-up nose.

"And what's that?" Principal Pollock asked.

"When Orlando started to announce at our first basketball game, everyone on the team responded by playing harder. It was amazing and we almost came back to win. Doing the play-by-play was his way of being a cheerleader on the bench. Orlando's a good kid, but I think the announcing has just gone a bit too far."

"A bit too far?" Mrs. Appleby shrieked.

Orlando winced at the high-pitched sound.

Principal Pollock sat forward. "This is a serious situation, young man."

Orlando nodded.

"Mrs. Appleby used to be one of our best math teachers before she retired a few years ago. Now, she may not substitute for a class you're in again."

Orlando looked down at his shoes.

"We can't have students disrespecting teachers and running wild in the classroom," the principal said sternly.

"I know."

"So, here's what's going to happen." Principal Pollock looked him directly in the eye, about to do a little announcing of her own.

Orlando braced himself for the bad news. He figured he might get a week of detentions in study hall after school. Or at worst have to do extra math homework every night for a week. That would be painful. But he wasn't ready for what he heard next.

"I believe the punishment should always fit the crime," Principal Pollock said. "So, starting this minute there'll be no more pretend radio announcing. Not in the classroom, not in the cafeteria, and not at any school basketball game. I don't ever want to hear the sound of your voice doing that again. And if I do, you will have played your last basketball game here at Evergreen Junior High. Am I making myself clear?"

Orlando looked up and nodded one last time. This broadcast was over.

★★★

Orlando didn't feel much like reading. He turned a few more pages of *Holes,* the novel he was reading for language-arts class, then put the book down on his bed-side table. He wanted to sleep but couldn't. He needed something to take his mind off what had gone down that morning in the principal's office. He turned off his bedroom light, reached for his headphones, and sat in the darkness staring at the glow of his laptop.

"HOOP Radio is live here at Madison Square Garden in the Big Apple, where Toronto is making it look easy to-night. The Raptors are out in front of the New York Knicks by a dozen and are starting to ham it up. The Knicks look asleep out there and the Raps would be wise not to wake them up. There's another Toronto alley-oop for two more and the Raptors players are rubbing it in by celebrating after each basket with a little dance. The crowd doesn't like it and neither do the Knicks."

Orlando realized he had forgotten to brush his teeth and so he got up and went down the hall to the bathroom. He figured the Raptors had the game un-der control and could survive without him listening for two minutes. There was no way they could blow a lead this big. Boy, was he wrong.

"What a turnaround, Todd!" he heard when he was back. *"Five buckets in a row and New York is back in the game! The crowd has come alive and is on its feet. Here come the Knicks again, hitting a three-point jumper from outside. And now the game is tied! We wondered if the Raptors showing off would fire up the Knicks and now we know — it did! Toronto can't buy a bucket and the Knicks are pouring them in."*

Orlando couldn't believe what he was hearing through his phones. *Showing off doesn't get you anywhere,* he thought.

"There's the final buzzer and the Raptors are walking off the court, losers. Toronto should have won this game. They had the respect of the Knicks until their showboating went too far. Way too far. They learned their lesson the hard way, Ted."

Orlando may not have been a professional basketball player, but tonight he knew exactly how they felt.

9 FIGHTING MAD

The Frontenac Falcons flew off the bus and into the Evergreen gym for their four-o'clock tilt against the Eagles. The court echoed with the sound of bouncing balls as the boys in the black sweatsuits started their shoot-around.

The Eagles were already warming up on their side of the court, eyeing their competition as they came in.

"We can take these guys," Zack said, banking a hook shot off the backboard.

"You know it!" Pete said, practicing both his left- and right-hand dribbling.

"They're no bigger or better than we are," Keegan chipped in, putting up a jumper.

"And just in case we fall behind, we've got our secret announcing weapon sitting on the bench," Cooper said. He pointed at Orlando.

"Yeah! Your play-by-play rocks, Double-O," Vijay said.

Orlando didn't feel like he rocked right now. He'd been down all day. He didn't want to talk to anyone and had steered clear of his teammates. He even ate lunch by himself at his locker instead of going into the cafeteria with the rest of the guys. He didn't want anyone to know his announcing days were over. Besides, he knew he'd been messing up on the court and didn't think that calling the play was enough of a reason to be on the team. And now that he couldn't announce, either, he figured his days were numbered.

"Let's bring it in!" Coach Krinski shouted.

In seconds, the players were huddled around him. "I've got three things to say, so listen up. One, we're tied in the standings with Frontenac, so this is a big game for us if we want to make the playoffs."

The players fist-bumped one another.

"Two, the starting line-up for today is Zack, Pete, Keegan, Cooper, and Vijay." Everyone nodded, knowing these were the best players they had. Around school they'd become known as the Fab Five.

"And three, there'll be no announcing from Orlando."

The Eagles looked bug-eyed with surprise.

"Except if we get behind, right, Coach?" Pete said.

"Not even if we're getting blown out by fifty points," Coach said.

"Why don't you want Double-O calling the game?" Keegan asked. "Orlando is the comeback kid."

"It's not up to me," Coach said. "This came all the way from the top — the principal's office."

"Old Lady Pollock," Cooper whispered under his breath.

The starting five walked slowly toward centre court, still stunned by the news. The four second-string players sat shaking their heads on the bench. Orlando slumped by himself a few feet away with his elbows on his knees and his chin on his hands. He stared into space. *What was the point in watching?* he asked himself. He probably wasn't going to play and couldn't even call the play-by-play to help his team.

The game didn't start well. From the opening tip the Falcons swooped around the Eagles with a fast-break offence that caught Zack and the team off guard. Cooper, Keegan, and the rest of the green-and-gold looked like they were running in sand.

The first half ended with the Eagles down by eight points. It could have been a blowout, but in the last minute, Pete got hot hitting a pair of three-point bombs from outside the arc.

Ten minutes into the second half the Frontenac coach called a time-out to bring in their second-string players. The Eagles were still stuck in neutral and the Falcons were in overdrive and pulling ahead. Coach Krinski took the opportunity to make a player change, as well.

"O'Malley, go in for Keegan."

Orlando was startled. Knowing he couldn't broadcast, he had practically been asleep on the bench. He stumbled onto the court and took his position at guard. Cooper passed him the ball, but he was still in a daze and the ball went sailing through his hands and out of bounds.

"Falcons' ball!" the ref said.

The Frontenac guard dribbled down Orlando's side of the court. Orlando thought he could make a steal and lunged for the ball, but the Falcon made a smooth crossover move and blew right by him on the way to the Eagles' basket for two more easy points.

The whistle blew again. "Keegan, you're back in!" Coach shouted. "Orlando, you're out."

Orlando moped on the bench for the rest of the game. Despite a late rally, the Eagles were shot down by the Falcons 57–48.

The locker room was as quiet as a classroom during an exam. Orlando sat as far away from Zack as he could. He felt sorry for himself. Coach had only played him for a minute. He got that. He didn't deserve to play more. Especially not after the hammer fell in the principal's office. His mom was still mad at him, too. He didn't feel like talking to anyone.

Orlando had just finished putting on his jeans and T-shirt when Zack sat down beside him. His normally easygoing face looked dead serious. "You're kind of letting us down, Double-O."

"Says who?"

"Me, Keegan, Cooper, Vijay . . . the whole team."

"Well, that's too bad," Orlando said, trying to talk tough.

"Yeah, it is. You had a good thing going and you blew it. Calling the game really pumped us up. You should have known better than to announce in a class. What were you thinking?"

Orlando thought it was bad enough getting lectured by the principal, but this was worse. Now, even his teammates had turned against him.

"Is that it? You done?"

Zack's face morphed into a smile. "Not quite. I wanted to invite myself over to shoot a few hoops again. Maybe help you with your game."

"You couldn't care less about my game," Orlando shot back.

"Not true," Zack said. "It would help the team."

"You just want to come over so you can shoot hoops with my sister," Orlando said, getting really angry now.

"I don't know what you're talking about."

"I think you do," Orlando said, spitting out the words. "I saw you looking over at the stands during the game. You were hoping Megan was there."

"I was looking for someone else."

"Yeah, right." Orlando was in Zack's face now. "Just like you were looking at her when she turned you inside out playing HORSE last weekend."

Now Zack was all up in Orlando's grille. "You're crazy."

"No, you're crazy . . . about Megan. I think she's the only reason you want to come over," Orlando shouted. "You're just using me!"

Orlando pushed Zack square in the chest with both hands. He'd had enough of his so-called friend. But Zack pushed right back, sending Orlando flying off the bench and onto the hard cement floor. Orlando came charging back with his arms spinning like an out-of-control windmill.

The fight was on.

Orlando swung wildly, hoping to land a punch. Zack's long, strong arms grabbed him by the shoulders and threw him to the floor again. The size difference between the boys was gigantic. It was David against Goliath — a one-sided UFC cage match between a fly-weight and a heavyweight. Zack sat on top of Orlando, pinning him to the cold, grey concrete.

Orlando squirmed, trying to escape. "Get off me, you overgrown loser!"

"The only loser here is you! You shouldn't even be playing."

"What are you guys doing?" Pete shouted as he ran over to break up the brawl.

It took three other teammates to pull Zack off Orlando. "We didn't think this would get so out of control," Keegan said.

"You guys are friends," Cooper said.

Orlando got up, his chest heaving. "Yeah, well, that's a funny way to treat a friend."

Zack stared down at Orlando and shook his head. "The truth is I was trying to be your friend. But you don't want the truth. All you want is attention."

The star centre threw on his backpack and walked out, leaving a silent locker room behind him.

10 LETTER PERFECT

Orlando had to read the email twice because he didn't believe it the first time.

Dear Mr. O'Malley,

Congratulations! You're the lucky winner of the HOOP Radio Courtside Contest. You've won an all-expense-paid trip for three to watch the Toronto Raptors play the Miami Heat. What does your trip include? Check out this fantastic list:

• VIA Rail tickets to Toronto

• Deluxe hotel room

• Dinner at the Raptors Club Restaurant

• Raptors vs Heat tickets

• Guest on the HOOP Radio broadcast with Todd and Ted

Your tickets for transportation and all

events will be sent to you later this
week. Have a great time!

Your friends at HOOP Radio

Orlando's eyes popped out of his head. He had never won anything before. Not unless you counted those goofy prizes that spill out of the crackers you pull apart with a loud bang at Christmas dinner.

He sat dazed in front of his laptop, picturing himself sitting courtside with the HOOP Radio announcers watching LeBron, Dwyane, and the rest of the Miami Heat players run by. It was so crazy, so unbelievable, he almost couldn't believe it himself.

If winning the contest was a surprise to Orlando, it was going to be a complete shock to his parents. They didn't even know he had entered.

Orlando was still wearing his pajamas when he raced into the kitchen and put his laptop on the table. His mom and sister were already dressed and finishing up their breakfasts. They were getting ready to go clothes shopping at the Kingston mall. Megan may have been a jock, but she was a stylish one. His dad wore a frayed brown robe and stood by the counter making waffles in the waffle iron, a Saturday-morning tradition in the O'Malley household. Orlando, Megan, and their mom had decided waffles were the only meal he was allowed to make, and that was only if he agreed to use the pre-mixed ingredients right out of the Aunt Jemima box.

They figured not much could go wrong.

"I've got news!" Orlando blurted.

"Yeah, yeah, we know the Raptors lost again," Megan said, not even looking up from her plate.

"That's not it, but this does have something to do with the Raptors."

"What, did they call you for a tryout or something?" She smirked.

"That's enough, Megs! Maybe they made a big trade or something," his dad said, spilling batter over the waffle iron.

"Wrong again, waffle king," Orlando joked. "I just won a trip to a Raptors game in Toronto!"

Now he had everyone's attention.

"And that's not all. I get to be a guest on the HOOP Radio broadcast with Todd and Ted!"

Orlando thought he had better come clean and explain things — so he told them how he had listened to the game one night and entered the contest. Then he showed his mom the email the radio station had sent him, so she could see it was the real deal.

"That's great news, Lando," his mom said, "but . . ."

"But what?" Orlando shot back, "I'm too small to go?"

"No, what about the no-announcing rule? Mrs. Pollock laid down the law."

"Mrs. Pollock can't lay down the law when it's nothing to do with school! I'm just going to be a guest on the show. Besides, I'm sure Todd and Ted won't ask me to announce. That's *their* job."

"When's the game?" his dad asked.

"Three weeks."

"And how many people is the trip for?" his mom asked.

"Three again," Orlando said, holding up his fingers.

"Megs, are you interested?" his dad asked.

Megan rolled her eyes. "What, in spending a whole weekend with announcer boy? You're kidding, right?"

"You're just jealous," Orlando said.

"Of you being an announcer? Not a chance. I'd rather be a player than some dumb guy who calls the play."

"Shut up! When I announced the game for the Eagles, it helped them. Ask anyone."

Megan pushed her plate away. "Whatev."

Orlando's mom broke in. "That's enough! Why don't I go with you, Lando? I haven't been home much lately, so this will give us a chance to catch up. Dad can stay home with Megan. That means there's one ticket left, so you can invite one of your friends."

Orlando's mood soured. He looked away from his mom.

"Who do you think might like going to a Raptors game with you?" she asked.

Orlando didn't know what to say. He didn't have any friends left on the basketball team and didn't know anyone else at his new school. "I'm not sure."

"What about that tall boy who shot hoops with you on the driveway a couple of weeks ago?" his mom suggested.

"Why don't you ask *Megan* his name?" Orlando sneered.

"I haven't a clue what his name is."

"You don't like Zack?"

"Was that his name? I thought it was geek."

★★★

For the next two weeks Orlando avoided Zack. He would walk the other way if he saw him in the hall and barely spoke to him during practice and games. He wanted to let things cool off between them and just couldn't make up his mind whether to invite him to the Raptors game or not. But if it wasn't Zack, he didn't know who it would be.

His behaviour didn't seem to bother Zack, though. He kept scoring and the Eagles began racking up the victories even without the announcing from Orlando, who spent more time on the bench than on the court. The team, in fact, had gone on a winning streak and finished the regular season with a 6–2 record, easily making the playoffs. Only their crosstown rivals, the Hilldale Hawks, finished ahead of them.

As the trip to Toronto got closer and closer, Orlando was forced to think more and more about his fight with

Zack. Had he jumped to conclusions? They'd been friends before Zack ever met his sister, hadn't they? And so what if Zack liked her? She couldn't care less about him. And maybe Zack was right about him not wanting to hear the truth. After all, Orlando didn't want to admit he'd made a mistake by announcing in class, and didn't want to admit that he wasn't good enough to play.

But what did it matter now? Zack hated his guts and probably wouldn't ever talk to him again.

It was the semifinal game of the playoffs, and the Eagles had just beaten the Bayridge Blazers by ten points. Orlando was changing back into his school clothes. He'd had a few minutes of playing time because Davis still wasn't back. And he had hit for a rare two points on a jumpshot from the top of the key. Man, it felt sweet! Orlando was relieved he'd finally helped the team with its scoring, since he wasn't able to help them with his announcing. Of course, his measly bucket was nothing compared to Zack's. The tall centre had poured in half of Evergreen's fifty-two points.

Orlando walked around the corner of the tall lockers to get a drink from the fountain, but stopped short when he saw that Zack was already there. "Sorry, I'll come back later."

"No need, I'm done," Zack said, wiping his mouth.

"Nice jumper, by the way."

"Nice twenty-six," Orlando said. "We're going to need plenty more of those in the final."

Orlando hadn't talked to Zack for some time, and even though the conversation was awkward he wanted to keep it going. He was tired of avoiding him.

"I see the Raptors are back in TO this weekend to play the Heat," Orlando said.

"It would be pretty cool to watch one of their games in person," Zack said.

"Yeah, it would," Orlando's tone was casual. "Do you want to go?"

Orlando couldn't believe what had just popped out of his mouth. He hadn't meant to say anything. But then again, he figured it was better to invite a teammate who may or may not like him than to go with just his mom. That would be lame.

Zack furrowed his brow. "What are you talking about?"

"You know that Courtside Contest on HOOP Radio?" Orlando asked.

"Yeah, the winner's going to be one lucky dude."

"Well, I'm that lucky dude."

"No way!"

"Way."

"When's the game?"

"This Saturday in Toronto."

"And you're asking me to go?" Zack said in surprise.

"I didn't think we were friends anymore."

"We weren't, but it's a basketball game and you like basketball."

"Let me think about it."

11 BEHIND DOOR NUMBER ONE

"I'll get it!" Orlando shouted as he walked into the hall to answer the doorbell. It was Friday night and he wasn't expecting anyone. He swung open the front door and was shocked to see who was standing there.

"Hey, Orlando," Zack said nervously.

Orlando looked up at the tall visitor. "You didn't have to come all the way over in person to tell me about going to the Raptors game. You could have texted me."

"I know, but telling you that I *would* like to go to the game isn't the only reason I'm here."

Orlando wondered what he meant. He did notice that Zack was dressed a lot more nicely than usual. He wore a black shirt with a collar instead of his usual T-shirt, and a new pair of blue jeans instead of his everyday ratty ones. He even had some kind of goop in his hair to make it stand up. "Why else would you be here?"

"Is that Zack?" Megan called from upstairs in her room.

"Yeah!" Orlando shouted, wondering how his sister would know.

"Tell him I'll be down in a minute. I'm just getting ready."

"You're here to see Megan?" Orlando asked.

"We're going to a movie."

"Really? I didn't think you liked her."

"I never said that."

Orlando did a slow burn. "That's the only reason I asked you to the Raptors game. Because I thought you were friends with me, not my stupid sister."

"Can't I be friends with both of you?" Zack asked.

"What's the problem, Orlando?" Megan said, coming down the stairs. The ponytail was gone and her hair was brushed and loose on her shoulders. Orlando could see makeup on her eyes and smell a whiff of perfume.

"It's your giant boyfriend."

"He's not my boyfriend."

"Then why are you going out with him?" Orlando said.

"Because he asked."

"I thought you didn't like him."

"I don't know if I like him or not. I haven't thought about it much."

"Well, start thinking about it, because he can only be friends with one of us," Orlando said steaming mad.

Mrs. O'Malley came smiling into the hallway. "Would someone like to introduce me to this good-looking guy?"

"No, no one wants to," Orlando said.

"This is Zack, Mom," Megan said. "He plays on Orlando's team."

"Why don't you come in and sit down?" his mom said, pointing to the fancy sofa in the living room that was usually reserved for adult guests. "There's Coke in the fridge."

"We were just leaving," Megan said, opening the front door and glaring at Orlando. "Let's go, Zack."

"Well, nice to meet you, Zack," Mom said.

"Yeah, it was super swell to meet you, Zack," Orlando said, aping his mom.

Orlando stood at the front door, not knowing what to think. It seemed like Zack was still using him just so he could see Megan. He should have seen this coming. But now it was too late to find another friend for the Raptors game. They were leaving tomorrow morning.

12 GREAT HEIGHTS

The VIA Rail train pulled out of Kingston Station at 9:50 a.m. sharp and headed west. The long chain of silver cars would wind along the north coast of Lake Ontario, passing Belleville and Oshawa on the way to its final destination — Union Station in downtown Toronto. Orlando settled into a high-backed seat that looked like it belonged on a jet, plugged in his iPod, and watched the countryside zip by. After seeing Zack and his sister walk out the front door on their date last night, talking to Zack was the last thing he wanted to do.

For the first half-hour of the trip there was an uneasy silence. To avoid looking at each other, both Orlando and Zack stared out the window listening to tunes while Mrs. O'Malley read a book.

Zack broke the ice. "Can't wait to see Dwyane Wade light it up tonight. He's the best."

Orlando shook his head. "Better than LeBron? Are you kidding me?"

"Well, I happen to think Wade is better."

"And I happen to think you don't know what you're talking about."

Mrs. O'Malley looked up from her book, annoyed by the arguing. "Well, I happen to think Derrick Rose of the Bulls is better than both of them. And so is the Thunder's Kevin Durant."

Orlando's jaw dropped and Zack's eyes popped.

"Wow! Mrs. O'Malley, you're like an NBA encyclopedia," Zack said.

"Yeah, where did you learn stuff like that?" Orlando asked.

"I read the sports pages. I listen to the news. I used to play hoops at university."

"Really?" Zack said. "But you're a chemistry professor."

"I am now, but there was a time when I wasn't sure which I wanted to do more — play basketball or study chemistry."

"What happened? I mean, how did you decide?" Zack asked as Orlando rolled his eyes, wondering why anyone would care.

"It became an easy decision when I realized I wasn't that good at basketball but really good at chemistry."

Orlando sat back in his chair. He knew his mom had played basketball for Queen's twenty years ago. One of the framed family photographs on the living-room mantel was of her wearing her gold uniform.

Soon the train hit the outskirts of Toronto, and Orlando could see the CN Tower gleaming in the sky. It was pretty hard to miss a 555-metre-high toothpick. As the train clacked closer to the station, he could see the tall office buildings downtown, the huge stadium where the Blue Jays played, and the Air Canada Centre — home of the Raptors.

As they walked to the hotel, Orlando's head bobbed and swiveled as he took in all the sights. Toronto was a lot bigger than his hometown, and a lot different. The sidewalk was filled with people wearing suits and walking in a hurry. But he also saw people just sitting on the sidewalk and in doorways. These people looked grubby and some of them held signs asking for money or food. One was a boy who couldn't have been much older than he was. He looked sad and angry at the same time. Orlando's mom reached into her purse and stopped to give him a couple of dollars for food. Orlando wondered why the boy wasn't at home with his parents. *Maybe he was an orphan who had never been adopted,* he thought.

Mrs. O'Malley opened the door to the hotel room and Orlando burst in, racing to the twenty-second-floor window to check out the view. "You can see everything from up here!"

"The lake's huge, but I can see across it from here!" Zack said.

"And the CN Tower is right beside us!" Orlando said, craning his neck to see the top.

"Man, if you think we're high here, imagine what it would be like up there!" Zack said.

"Why don't we find out?" Orlando's mom said. "The Raptors game doesn't start until seven tonight, so we can visit the tower this afternoon."

★★★

Zack stood gazing skyward at the tower. "My neck hurts just looking up."

"Yeah, but I have to look up even farther," Orlando, almost a foot shorter, said.

"Let's go up to the Glass Floor," Orlando said reading the sign listing the different viewing areas you could visit.

"Are you sure you want to do that?" his mom asked a little nervously.

"Yeah, I don't know," Zack said. "It's pretty high. I read there are 1,776 steps to get all the way up there."

"It's not like we're walking. Let's go," Orlando said impatiently.

Orlando stepped off the elevator and looked around. There was blue sky as far as his eyes could see. It was like looking out the window of a plane.

"There's the Glass Floor!" Orlando said, pointing to the special area of the observation deck.

Orlando and his mom put one foot in front of the other and started inching their way across the clear, see-through floor. The cars driving by underneath looked like toys, and the people walking along the sidewalk looked like ants.

"It's hard to look down, isn't it, Zack?"

Orlando didn't hear a reply.

"Zack?"

When Orlando looked over his shoulder, he saw Zack still standing on the edge of the Glass Floor. He hadn't taken a single step. He seemed frozen in place and was looking to his left and his right, anyplace but down.

"I'm not feeling so great," Zack said, looking a little pale. "Maybe I'll just wait here."

For the first time Orlando realized he could do something that Zack couldn't. *You can't be a star at everything,* he thought.

Orlando's mom looked a little white in the face herself. "Let's go back to the hotel and relax before the game," she said.

"Good idea, Mrs. O," Zack said, pushing the elevator down button as fast as he could.

13 LOST AND FOUND

Orlando checked his watch — 6:30 p.m. That was the exact time HOOP Radio had told them to meet at the Air Canada Centre. He pulled open the big glass door for his mom and Zack. Waiting for them just inside the doorway was a young woman wearing a Raptors red shirt and pants. She had short dark hair and held a white sign with the word "O'Malley" written on it in big black letters.

"You must be looking for us," Orlando said. "We're the O'Malleys. Except for this guy. He's a Jackson."

The woman flashed a huge smile with super-white teeth, "Hi, I'm Marni from HOOP Radio and I'll be your host tonight."

"Are we going straight to the broadcast booth?" Orlando asked eagerly.

"We'll visit the HOOP Radio broadcast booth in the second half of the game," Marni said. "But first, is anyone hungry?"

"I could eat a horse," Orlando said.

"Then follow me."

After a short elevator ride Marni walked down a long white hallway where pictures of famous Raptors hung on the walls. She opened the two large crimson doors of the Raptors Club Restaurant and took them over to a booth with huge red leather seats. Orlando wasn't ready for what he saw next.

"Man, that is so sick!" he said, pointing to the floor-to-ceiling windows. "You can see the entire arena!"

"We can watch the game and eat at the same time," Zack said, eager to start two of his most-favourite things in the world.

Orlando's mom nodded. "And I can just relax and leave the cooking to someone else."

Zack, Orlando, and his mom stared out the window in amazement. From where they sat high up in the arena they could look down over the 18,000 seats that surrounded the basketball court. There were screens everywhere flashing bright signs urging the crowd to MAKE SOME NOISE and cheer on the Raptors. Pounding through the loudspeakers and straight into Orlando's ears was music driven by a heavy drumbeat. He wasn't sure if he was at a basketball game or a rock concert.

The ref was at centre court just about to toss up the opening tip between the Raptors and the Miami Heat. The Raptors were wearing their white home uniforms while the Heat were dressed in the menacing black tops and shorts they wore when playing on the road. Orlando took a big bite of his Backcourt Burger, stuffed a Fast Break Fry into his mouth, and took a pull on the two straws sticking out of his Monster Jam Milkshake. This was the best meal of his life!

The atmosphere inside the arena was electric. Orlando knew the crowd was totally into the game, cheering whenever the Raptors scored and gasping in amazement whenever Wade or LeBron drove to the basket. The lead see-sawed back and forth in the first half and ended in a 55–55 tie.

Orlando studied the dessert menu. He didn't know if he could eat another bite, but he was going to try.

"I'll have the Backboard Banana Sundae," he said to the waitress.

"I'll try the Pump Fake Pie," Zack said, holding his bulging stomach.

The boys were halfway through their desserts when Marni flashed her white smile into the red booth again.

"You guys ready for a little play-by-play action with HOOP Radio?"

"Perfect timing," Orlando said, putting down his spoon. "I was so full I couldn't finish anyway."

Orlando left his mom sitting in the restaurant drinking her coffee while he and Zack followed Marni down the elevator to the main floor.

"We're going through the huge food court where all the pizza, fries, and pop are sold. It's halftime, so it's going to be a real zoo with fans grabbing snacks. You better stay close."

A few steps later Orlando was hit by a wall of sights, sounds, and smells. Thousands of hungry fans passed before his eyes, thumping music pounded his ears, and the smell of freshly buttered popcorn wafted into his nose. It was a complete five-sense basketball-o-rama experience!

"Can you guys wait here?" Orlando yelled over the crowd noise. "I've got to find a washroom."

"Way over there," Marni shouted, pointing across the jam-packed hall.

"Hey, want me to go with you?" Zack asked.

"Forget it," Orlando called over his shoulder, disappearing into the sea of fans.

A couple of minutes later Orlando cruised out of the washroom, then stopped dead in his tracks. If it was possible, there were even more people sardined into the hall than before. He searched the crowd looking for Zack and Marni, but all he could see were belt buckles and shirts. There was no way he could see above the crush of people. He was trapped.

Orlando made his best guess where he had come from and started snaking through the crowd, looking for Zack. No luck. When he got to the spot he thought they were, he was still surrounded by swarms of complete strangers. *Where can they have gone?* he wondered.

Worry turned to panic. He pushed his way through the flood of fans to one of the big gates that led into the seating area of the main arena. No Zack, no Marni.

Orlando's heart raced. *What should I do?* He fought his way back against the stream of spectators coming into the main hall and waited.

Did Zack and Marni go ahead without me? Orlando wondered. *Would Zack take advantage of the situation? Maybe he wanted to see the announcers at HOOP Radio all by himself. Maybe Zack was going to pretend he won the contest. Pretend he was me. How would Todd and Ted know the difference?* Orlando's head swirled with crazy thoughts. "I knew I couldn't trust him," he said out loud.

The words were hardly out of his mouth when Orlando spotted a familiar face above all the other faces in the crowd. He'd never been so happy to see the tall centre. Zack's head swivelled like an owl's scanning every which way for Orlando. Marni was no doubt beside him but was far too short to be of any help on this search-and-rescue mission.

Orlando waved his arms over his head. "I'm over here!"

"Thank goodness we found you," Marni said when they'd made their way to him. "We were worried sick."

"No big deal," Orlando said, hiding his fear.

"We better stick together from now on," Zack said.

"You mean it?"

Zack nodded. "That's what friends do."

★★★

Inside the main arena electronic signs flashed neon messages around the entire lower bowl while the huge Jumbotron scoreboard hung over centre court and re-played video highlights of all the best plays of the game. The crowd chanted *Go Raptors Go* while the music blasted from giant speakers overhead. Orlando had to cover his ears until he got used to it.

With Marni in the lead, Orlando followed Zack as they zigzagged between all the spectators until they came to the row of broadcasters sitting right beside the court. Just a few metres in front of them were Todd and Ted, announcing the game live for HOOP Radio.

"Pull up a chair, guys," Todd said, pointing to the two empty seats beside them.

Orlando sat down just as LeBron James ran by so close Orlando could almost reach out and touch the flaming-red basketball logo on his Miami Heat's black jersey. Orlando and Zack looked at each other in amazement.

Ted handed the boys headphones. "Put these on so you can hear all the action."

Orlando was happy to put on the phones. Now he could block out some of the crowd noise and hear Todd better. Each headset had a microphone attached in front for speaking. He listened to Todd call the game.

"THE HEAT HAVE CALLED A TIME-OUT WITH JUST A MINUTE LEFT TO PLAY AND THE SCORE DEADLOCKED AT A HUNDRED POINTS. AND THAT GIVES US A CHANCE TO INTRODUCE THE WINNER OF THE BIG HOOP RADIO

COURTSIDE CONTEST — ORLANDO O'MALLEY FROM KINGSTON, ONTARIO. SAY HI TO THE THOUSANDS OF RAPTORS FANS LISTENING TO TONIGHT'S GAME FROM ALL OVER NORTH AMERICA, ORLANDO."

Thousands of fans? All over North America? Orlando had never thought about how many people tuned in to a HOOP Radio broadcast. He always just plugged in and listened to Todd and Ted as if they were talking only to him. Now his mouth was so sawdust dry he could hardly speak.

"Hi," Orlando croaked.

"Why don't you tell everyone the name of your high school basketball team?"

Orlando was so nervous he couldn't remember the name. He glanced at Zack and read the name on his green team jacket.

"The Evergreen Eagles," he said at the last second.

"And tell us, Orlando, who's your favourite team in the NBA?"

Orlando had never thought about what team he liked the best. Sure, he listened to the Raptors games, but he liked other teams, too. He didn't answer at first.

"I bet we can guess," Ted said, breaking the silence. "It wouldn't happen to be that other team from Florida, would it? You know, the one where Disneyworld is."

"You mean the *Orlando* Magic?" said Orlando.

"Makes sense, don't you think? O-r-l-a-n-d-o?" Todd laughed.

Orlando didn't really like the Magic, but he could see how Todd might think so, Orlando having the same name and everything. Besides, too much dead air had gone by and he knew he had to say something fast.

"Yeah, that's it."

"Well, Orlando 'Magic' O'Malley, how would you like to call a little play-by-play of this game?"

Orlando shot a wide-eyed look at Zack. What should he do? The real announcers at HOOP Radio were asking him to call the game in front of thousands, maybe millions of fans. He knew he'd never get another chance like this in his life.

"Go for it, Double O," Zack said. "Principal Pollock never said anything about announcing a Raptors game."

"Let's do this!" Orlando said, his voice suddenly booming. He pulled up his chair even with Todd and Ted and adjusted his microphone.

"LET'S SET THE STAGE, HOOP FANS. WE'RE IN THE FINAL MINUTE OF A CLASSIC SHOWDOWN WITH THE HEAT TRAILING THE HOMETOWN RAPTORS BY A SINGLE BUCKET. AFTER THE TIME-OUT, BOSH THROWS THE BALL IN TO WADE, WHO DISHES IT TO JAMES, CUTTING INTO THE PAINT. LEBRON ONE-HANDS THE ROCK AND TAKES IT TO THE HOLE FOR A MONSTER SLAM! WE HAVE OURSELVES A TIE BALL GAME. LOOKS LIKE WE'RE HEADED FOR OVERTIME!"

The two HOOP Radio hosts smiled and shook their heads in disbelief. "That is one great voice you have there, Magic," Todd said.

"I'd say an announcing star has been born." Ted grinned.

Orlando handed the headset back and listened to his two heroes continue with the broadcast.

"You're listening to the Todd, Ted, *and* Magic show on HOOP Radio."

14 THE VOLUNTEER

"Here comes the Magic man!" "You know the score, Magic."

"Nice play-by-play, Magic."

"When's the next Magic show?"

Orlando walked down the hall to his locker Monday morning listening to all the shout-outs. They came flying in from every corner of the school. From kids standing at their lockers to teachers passing by on their way to class. The funny thing was, he didn't know any of the people saying them. Orlando thought this must be how NBA stars felt when fans called out their name on the street or in a restaurant as if they knew them.

Of course, there was one person at the school Orlando didn't hear anything from. Principal Pollock wasn't exactly rushing out of her office to high-five him for his HOOP Radio appearance. He wondered whether she had heard about his announcing at the Raptors game. Not that she could do much about it, but he didn't need another lecture, especially not today.

From the moment he got up this morning, Orlando had been a bundle of nerves. There was no escape from thinking about this afternoon's game. He'd walk down the corridor and see hand-painted, green-and-yellow posters encouraging the Eagles to "Hoop it Up!" He'd walk past the gym and hear the cheerleaders practicing, "Hawks, Hawks, you're all done . . . Eagles, Eagles, we're number one!" Every time he saw Pete, Keegan, Cooper, and Vijay, they'd exchange silent nods, recognizing that everyone was too tense to talk.

Orlando sat in every class twitching like a dog with a bad case of fleas. When the final bell of the final class rang, he sprinted to the gym to get ready for the game. The championship game. Orlando had never played in a game this big and his stomach was doing somersaults. He had to settle down.

Orlando glanced up at the clock in the change room — 3:30. He felt better knowing that game time was just half an hour away. Waiting seemed a lot more nerve-wracking than actually playing. He sat between Keegan and Cooper and looked around. Vijay and Zack were getting dressed in front of their lockers. But they weren't alone. There was someone else sitting on the bench he hadn't seen in weeks — Davis. And he was wearing his uniform! Orlando had known Davis was coming back but didn't think he'd be playing in this game.

"I need your attention," Coach Krinski said. "I have some good news and some bad news."

The somersaults in Orlando's stomach were turning into a full-fledged gymnastics routine with cartwheels and flips.

"The good news is that Davis is back from his broken arm. I saw him shoot some baskets before school today and he's ready to go. Davis is one of our best players and we'll need him out there today."

Orlando bit his lower lip, expecting the worst.

Coach Krinski paced in front of the team. "The bad news is that we can only play a total of ten men, which means one of you has to sit out. I could make the decision myself, but first I'm asking for a volunteer to do it for the team."

The room was silent.

Orlando knew it couldn't be Zack or Pete or Keegan or Cooper or Vijay or any of the other guys on the team. They were all too valuable. He finally had to admit to himself why he wasn't scoring many baskets or getting much playing time during the games. It wasn't because he was too short — he was always using that as an excuse. It was because he wasn't *good* enough. He was a lot better at firing up the team with his announcing — if only he was still allowed to do it. But he had gone too far in the classroom and had to pay the price.

Orlando raised his hand. "I volunteer, Coach."

"You're a big man, Orlando," Coach said, looking him straight in the eye.

Coach Krinski continued to address the troops before the big battle. "There are going to be a lot of extra fans out there today, so let's put on a good show. I'm sure many of your parents will be making a special effort to attend."

Orlando figured he didn't have to worry about that. He had mentioned the big game to his parents, but didn't expect them to show up, especially since it was being played in the afternoon. He knew his mom would be hard at work finishing her chemistry experiment in the lab. His dad ran like a clock. He went to the university and returned home the same time every day. Orlando didn't think anything could change his routine. Now that he wasn't playing in the game, Orlando hoped his parents didn't make an appearance anyway.

Coach Krinski stood in the middle of the room while the other players finished lacing up their shoes. "This is it, gentlemen. This is why we played hard all season — to have the chance to play in the final game and be called city champions."

"We can do this!" Keegan called from the back of the room.

Coach shifted his gaze. "Earlier in the year the Hawks beat us by just a single point. It could have gone either way. And today it's going to go our way."

"Just one point!" Cooper shouted.

"Let's do this for Evergreen Junior High!" Pete called.

"Let's do this for Magic!" Zack said.

"For Magic!" the team shouted in unison.

Coach slowly turned around the room. "We're going to play tough but we're going to play fair. I want to see the ball going inside to Zack as much as possible. It worked for us during the season and it's going to work for us today."

"Eagles!" Vijay shouted.

"Eagles!" Davis joined in.

"Eagles!" cheered the rest of the team, now standing and chanting.

Orlando cheered, too, but his heart wasn't really in it. He finished taking off the green-and-gold uniform he was so proud of and put his school clothes back on again.

15 FIRST-HALF BLUES

The Eagles flooded out of the locker room and into the gym like a green-and-gold wave. Orlando could hear the cheers from the crowd in the stands and from the cheerleaders on the sidelines. Half the spectators were for the Eagles and the other half were Hawks supporters who'd come by bus from their school in Hilldale.

Orlando knew he wasn't going to play, but he still wanted to sit on the bench with the rest of the team. He stayed focused on the Eagles taking their layups and didn't once look back into the stands. He did sneak a peek at the other end of the court to see the Hawks doing their own warm-up drills. The first-place team in the red uniforms looked relaxed and some were even joking. Orlando hoped they were overconfident and wouldn't be ready for the Eagles.

"Hey pipsqueak!" a voice called from behind him. "Isn't there a height restriction for this game?

"Yeah, like for an amusement-park ride?" another said.

Orlando turned around to see two Hawks standing not ten feet away, pointing and laughing at him.

"He's so small he must be the team mascot."

The two hecklers backed away when the tallest Eagle in the gym came racing over. "Ignore them, Orlando," Zack said. "We'll see who's laughing at the end of the game."

Orlando didn't want anyone to fight his battles for him, but was glad Zack was on his side.

Coach Krinski called the boys in for one last huddle.

"Let's give it all we've got, guys. One . . . two . . . three . . . Eagles!"

The starting five took the floor. Zack at centre, Pete and Davis at forward, with Keegan and Cooper backing them up at guard. Orlando knew it was a good line-up. He just didn't know if it was good *enough*. He sat on the bench and studied the Hawks taking their positions for the opening tip. They all looked big. Even their centre matched up with Zack, and Orlando watched them stare each other down like two boxers in a ring. Orlando hoped the Eagles had the knockout punch.

The ref launched the ball in the air with the tip going to the Hawks. Their speedy guard brought the ball into Eagles territory before passing deep into the corner. As soon as the Hawks forward got the ball, he threw it to their big man standing at the high post in front of the basket. The big guy faked left, then dribbled right, blowing around Zack and putting the ball up off the backboard and through the hoop for the first two points of the game.

Orlando thought the Eagles looked tight but figured they'd come roaring back. Cooper threw the ball in from behind the basket. He aimed for Keegan, who was cutting across the middle, but the ball went right through his fingertips and into the waiting hands of a red-shirted Hilldale guard. The Hawks had it again! There was a quick toss to their forward in the other corner, who put up a long jumper from behind the three-point line, and it was 5–0 just like that. The game was barely a minute old and the Eagles were already in trouble.

Orlando shook his head and shot a glance at the crowd. In the half of the stands where everyone was wearing green, he couldn't believe what he saw. Sitting side by side were his mom and dad! They had actually listened to him when he'd told them about the game and left work early just to be here. At first he was glad and then quickly realized they'd see he wasn't playing. Now he was embarrassed and it wasn't just because of the score.

For the rest of the first half the Hawks continued to run and gun. Their guards moved the ball fast and hit the open man every time they pushed down the court. Their forwards were shooting the lights out from outside, and their inside game seemed to be unstoppable with their big, bruising centre outmuscling Zack on every possession.

The Eagles fought back as best they could. Orlando thought Keegan and Cooper were the two best Eagles on the court, snaking through the Hawks defence and putting up shots that found the basket from just outside the paint. But having only the Eagle guards score wasn't nearly enough. They needed Pete and Davis to find the net from the corners and Zack had to find his groove in the middle. If they didn't, this was going to be one long afternoon.

As the clock ticked down Orlando slouched on the bench, wishing he could do something to give the team a lift. He knew he couldn't play, but he wished he could at least call the play-by-play. But there was no way that was going to happen. He could see Principal Pollock in the crowd. He figured she must be just glaring at him and not even watching the game.

The buzzer sounded to end the first half. The Eagles looked like a team that was already defeated. Orlando and the rest of his teammates trudged off the court while staring up at the scoreboard: HAWKS 34–EAGLES 20.

16 LOCKER SHOCKER

The Eagles sat slumped in their change room. No one said a word. They had ten minutes before the second half started — ten minutes to figure out how to turn the game around. Coach Krinski seemed just as dejected as the players, but he put on a brave face.

"It's not over yet, guys. There's still time."

"Yeah, time for them to score even more," Pete said from the corner.

"We need a new game plan," Zack said. "They're shutting me down inside."

"We need to be looser," Keegan said. "You can't shoot when you're tight."

"What we really need is some Magic," Cooper said, turning to Orlando.

"Yeah, a little play-by-play magic would pump us up," Vijay agreed.

"Give that dream up," Pete said. "Old Lady Pollock isn't going to change her mind."

Just then the door to the change room swung open

and in walked a visitor no one expected. Every jaw in the room dropped.

It was Old Lady Pollock herself!

"Seems like you boys need a pep talk," the principal said, looking around the room. "But I'm not the one to give it."

All eyes were fixed on the grey-haired woman in the green sweater standing in the middle of the change room. The *boys'* change room!

Principal Pollock put her hands on her hips. "Mr. O'Malley, I'm here to consider lifting your suspension on calling the play-by-play of Eagle games."

The room exploded with claps, whistles, and hoots. "All right!"

Coach Krinski looked on, just as surprised by the principal's appearance as the players.

"But I want to tell you why I've changed my mind," Mrs. Pollock went on, still looking at Orlando. "You see, I happened to overhear the Raptors game Mr. Pollock was listening to on Saturday night and you can imagine my surprise when I heard a familiar voice doing the play-by-play at the end of the game. But my surprise wasn't that you were announcing, it was how good you were. You have real talent."

Every eye in the room remained laser-focused on the principal.

"Then when I saw that you had voluntarily taken yourself out of today's game, the biggest game of the year, well, I thought that was a big sacrifice to make on behalf of the team.

The principal smiled. "So, from this moment on you can announce again. Your team needs you. But you have to promise me, Mr. O'Malley, that you only announce in the games, and you only announce in the gymnasium. Not in the hallway, not in the cafeteria, and most certainly not in the classroom. Am I making myself clear?"

Orlando sat in silence, still getting over the shock of seeing the principal standing just a few feet away. Orlando finally managed to squeeze out a couple of words.

"Yes, ma'am."

The principal gave a nod to Coach and turned toward the door. She glanced back, her gaze serious. "Old Lady Pollock," she said, "is going to leave now, but before she does, she has one more important order for you to follow."

The room fell silent one more time.

"Let's kick some butt out there!"

17 MAGIC TIME

The Eagles blasted out of the change room. The players charged across the floor, jumping and slapping one another on the back. "We can do it!" "Let's go, boys!" "This is our game!"

Orlando looked across at the Hilldale half of the court. The Hawks had stopped their warm-up in its tracks and just watched their competition. The Hawks didn't seem to know what to make of this crazy pack of basketball players in the green-and-gold uniforms. This wasn't the same team of low-flying Eagles they'd faced in the first half.

Orlando looked in the stands. Mrs. Pollock had returned to her seat and was clapping and cheering along with the rest of the crowd, who had picked up on the Eagles' new-found energy. A few feet away his parents made eye contact with Orlando for the first time that afternoon. Both his mom and dad waved excitedly and gave him a thumbs-up. Orlando knew they would cheer for him no matter whether he played or not. He didn't feel embarrassed anymore. He was ready to go.

The ref tossed the ball in the air to start the second half. That was the only signal Orlando needed.

"ZACK, THE BIG EAGLES CENTRE, GOES HIGH, EASILY WINNING THE JUMP AND SWATS THE BALL BACK TO HIS LIGHTNING-FAST GUARD. PETE HURLS THE BALL DOWN COURT TO A STREAKING VIJAY, WHO BREAKS FOR THE BASKET AND HAULS IN THE BALL WITH ONE HAND, TAKES TWO LONG STEPS, AND LAYS IT IN SMOOTH LIKE BUTTER. TWO POINTS FOR THE EAGLES!"

The crowd erupted in cheers.

"THE EAGLES HAVE THE HAWKS PENNED IN THEIR OWN ZONE WITH A FULL-COURT PRESS. THEY'RE BUZZING AROUND THE HAWKS LIKE A SWARM OF YELLOW JACKETS. IN DESPERATION THE HAWKS TRY TO PASS, BUT IT'S INTERCEPTED BY DAVIS, WHO MAKES A BEELINE FOR THE HOLE AND BANKS IT IN FOR THE DEUCE!"

The Eagle players watching from the sideline stood up. All eyes were on the court. All ears were on the small guy with the big voice sitting on the end of the bench.

"THE HAWKS FINALLY PUSH THE BALL OVER THE CENTRE LINE AND INTO EAGLES TERRITORY. THEY LOOK CAUTIOUS, HESITANT, AND DON'T KNOW WHAT TO DO. PETE AND VIJAY ARE WAVING THEIR HANDS LIKE WINDMILLS. THE HAWKS GUARD CAN'T SEE WHO TO PASS TO. HE PANICS AND THROWS THE BALL AWAY. COOPER GRABS THE LOOSE BALL AND DRIBBLES DOWN COURT. HE SPOTS ZACK POSTING UP ON THE EDGE OF THE

KEY AND FLICKS THE ROCK TO HIS TALL CENTRE. ZACK TAKES A STEP TO HIS RIGHT, EXTENDS HIS LONG ARM AND LAUNCHES A SKY HOOK THAT SAILS THROUGH THE AIR, CATCHING NOTHING BUT NET! THE EAGLES ARE ON A SIX-ZERO RUN. THIS GAME IS FAR FROM OVER, LADIES AND GENTLEMEN."

The game continued at a frenzied pace. Up and down, and up and down the court. Both teams were running on adrenaline. Drops of sweat were flying everywhere. Out of the corner of his eye Orlando could see the green tops of the Eagle cheerleaders. The girls stood along the edge of the court clapping and shouting.

"Here we go, Eagles, here we go!"

"DAVIS TAKES THE PASS FROM PETE WAY OUTSIDE THE ARC AND LAUNCHES A LONG THREE-POINTER FROM DOWNTOWN. AND I MEAN ALL THE WAY FROM PRINCESS STREET IN DOWNTOWN KINGSTON. THAT BALL WENT UP SO HIGH IT CAME DOWN WET. AND HE NAILS IT. WHAT A SHOT! THE EAGLES ARE WITHIN EIGHT."

While most of the Eagles had found a higher gear, Zack still seemed stuck in first. He was trying his best, but Orlando knew he wasn't playing like he could. Like he'd played all year.

Orlando quickly scanned the crowd. The stands were all filled except for the top row. Those seats had been empty all game — until now. To Orlando's shock a lone girl with long blond hair and an all-too-familiar face was sitting there. It was Megan! *She must have snuck in at halftime when we were in the change room,* Orlando thought. *Is she here to watch me or Zack?* Orlando didn't know and couldn't worry about it now. He shifted his eyes back to the play just in time to see Zack pick up his game.

"NOW THE SLEEPING GIANT IS AWAKE! THE TALL CENTRE HAS BEEN THE LEADER OF THIS TEAM ALL SEASON AND SUDDENLY HE'S PLAYING LIKE IT. LOOK AT THE BIG MAN GO. HE'S GOT STEEL IN HIS EYES AND FIRE IN HIS BELLY. COOPER FEEDS ZACK THE BALL UNDER THE HAWKS BASKET. HIS LONG FINGERS WRAP AROUND THE ROCK. HE TURNS TO FACE HIS DEFENDER, ALMOST DARING HIM TO STOP HIM. BUT THERE'S NO DENYING THE EAGLES CAPTAIN. THE HAWKS DEFENDER LUNGES FOR THE BALL AND ZACK SCHOOLS HIM WITH A MOVE TO THE LEFT. HE PUTS THE BALL ON THE FLOOR FOR ONE DRIBBLE, THEN LAYS IT UP AND OFF THE GLASS FOR TWO MORE. THE TOWER OF POWER IS BACK!"

After making his two points Zack made a slight detour. Instead of running back up the middle of the court, he ran along the sideline and pointed at Orlando. Orlando gave a big grin and pointed right back.

The Eagles had made an incredible comeback and were only down by a single point. They were so close to catching the Hawks they could almost taste it. They still had to slow down the Hilldale scoring, though. It was great that Zack, Pete, Vijay, Cooper, and Davis were finding the bottom of the net, but to win the game they had to stop the big red machine. Sometimes to keep the Hawks from going to the hoop, the Eagles were forced to foul their powerful opponents.

"HERE COME THE HAWKS AGAIN. THEY'RE TRYING TO BREAK THROUGH THE BRICK WALL OF THE EAGLES DEFENCE. THEY SPOT AN OPENING. THE HAWKS WINGMAN GRABS THE ROCK AND SLASHES TOWARD THE BASKET. COOPER IS OUT OF POSITION AND HACKS THE SPEEDY HAWKS FORWARD ON THE ARM TO STOP THE SHOT. THE REF BLOWS THE WHISTLE. THE HAWKS PLAYER TAKES TWO FREE THROWS, BUT HE'S WOUND TIGHTER THAN A RUBBER BAND AND MISSES THEM BOTH. THE EAGLES ARE STILL ONLY DOWN BY ONE!"

Not wasting a second, Coach Krinski looked at the referee and formed a "T" with the palms of his hands. A time-out was called, and the Eagle players huddled around Coach, waiting to hear the next move.

"There's under a minute left in the game," Coach said. "We've got to get the ball to Zack in the middle for the score. Great job, Orlando! Keep pumping us up!"

Zack thrust his fist into the circle. Pete, Keegan, Cooper, Vijay, Orlando, and the rest of the team did the same.

"Time for a little magic," Zack said, nodding at Orlando. "One . . . two . . . three . . . Eagles!"

Orlando was so nervous he wasn't sure he could keep talking. He took the few steps back to the bench and was relieved his brain was still sending signals to his wobbly legs. He shot a glance into the stands and saw his parents smiling back at him. A few rows up he could hear Megan shouting his name. Finally he spotted Principal Pollock waving at him down below. He may not have been on the court, but he still had fans cheering for him.

Every nerve in Orlando's body tingled. His heart pounded, his throat went dry, and he couldn't swallow. He had to find a way to keep announcing. He couldn't freak out. That wasn't going to help the team. The ref blew the whistle to start the game again. Orlando took a swig from his water bottle and began to call the play-by-play.

"HERE WE GO, BASKETBALL FANS. THE FINAL MINUTE OF THE CITY CHAMPIONSHIP. IT ALL COMES DOWN TO THIS. THE UNDERDOG EVERGREEN EAGLES HAVE FOUGHT THEIR WAY BACK AGAINST THE HIGHLY FAVOURED HILLDALE HAWKS AND ARE JUST A SINGLE POINT AWAY FROM WINNING THIS UNFORGETTABLE GAME AND SENDING THE CROWD INTO A FRENZY! PETE THROWS IN THE BALL FROM THE SIDELINE TO DAVIS, WHO FLIPS IT TO COOPER, WHO DRIBBLES IT UP COURT. THIRTY SECONDS TO PLAY. THE FLASHY EAGLES GUARD IS ACROSS CENTRE AND INTO THE HAWKS ZONE. HE'S BEING COVERED LIKE A BLANKET BY THE HAWKS DEFENDER BUT FINDS A WAY TO BOUNCE A PASS TO THE BIG MAN IN THE MIDDLE. ZACK HAS THE

ROCK. EVERYBODY KNOWS HE WANTS TO SHOOT. THE HAWKS KNOW, THE CROWD KNOWS, EVEN THE REFEREES KNOW. JUST TEN SECONDS ON THE CLOCK. ZACK IS BEING DOUBLE COVERED BUT THE BIG MAN, THE HEART OF THE EAGLES SQUAD, WILL NOT BE DENIED. JUST THREE SECONDS LEFT. ZACK GOES HIGH IN THE AIR ABOVE HIS DEFENDERS AND RELEASES THE JUMP SHOT. THE AIR IN SLOW MOTIONSLOW MOTION . . . AND . . . SWISH! IT'S EAGLES 50–49!"

18 WAFFLING

Orlando slid into the kitchen with a hunger in his stomach the size of Lake Ontario. Luckily, it was Saturday morning and he knew what that meant. Waffles! He sat at the table watching his dad, who was wearing his mom's pink apron and attempting to pour flour into a big bowl.

"THIS IS GOING TO SURPRISE A LOT OF YOU WAFFLE FANS OUT THERE, BUT THIS MORNING BIG DADDY O'MALLEY IS AT THE COUNTER MIXING UP ANOTHER HUMONGOUS BOWL OF BATTER. THAT'S RIGHT, YOU HEARD ME. DESPITE THE HUGE MESS HE MADE LAST TIME HE'S GOING TO GIVE IT ANOTHER TRY. HE PICKS UP THE BOWL AND STARTS POURING THE GOOPY LIQUID

INTO THE HOT WAFFLE IRON, BUT OH NO! HE DOESN'T KNOW WHEN TO STOP AND WE HAVE AN OVERFLOW SITUATION OF MAJOR PROPORTIONS. THERE'S ONLY ONE SOLUTION. CALL MOM!"

Still wearing her blue housecoat, Orlando's mom hurried into the kitchen to provide some emergency waffle aid. She wasn't empty-handed, though. She was carrying the same round object wrapped in bright green paper that Orlando hadn't seen for weeks.

"You may not have thought you deserved this at the beginning of the season," she said, smiling, "but even you have to admit you've earned it now."

Orlando still wasn't sure he had. After all, it was Zack who'd sunk the winning basket. All Orlando had done was cheer on the team by announcing the play-by-play. Everyone seemed to appreciate his effort, though. Principal Pollock gave him a big hug after the game, and during the intercom announcements the following morning, Coach Krinski had made a special shout-out to the whole school thanking Orlando for a job well done.

But it was what his mom and dad said in the car on the way home that he remembered the most. They'd told him it was the best weekday afternoon they had ever spent — better than any afternoon in the lab or office at the university. And from now on they'd be coming home from work on time because Orlando and Megan deserved it.

Orlando realized he was lucky to have parents who wanted to come home to see him. He thought about the poor kids in the orphanages in Haiti and the boy on the street in Toronto, and wondered if anyone came to see them.

Orlando was so hungry he didn't know whether he should open the wrapped gift or dive into the plate his dad had just slid in front of him. He took one look at the waffle, shaped like a two-headed alien, and quickly chose the gift.

"I wonder what it is?" He laughed as he ripped open the green paper that covered the official NBA ball. Orlando felt good knowing his parents had got him the ball because they wanted to, not because he'd demanded it.

As he finally tucked in to his waffle, his dad said, "You should go shoot some hoops by yourself on the driveway."

"Or I could change into my old uniform and show you some of my slick moves," his mom said, pretending to dribble around the kitchen. "I was pretty good in my day."

Orlando rolled his eyes. "I have a better idea."

★★★

Zack made one dribble on the pavement, then took one long step around Orlando before going airborne and laying the new ball off the backboard and into the basket.

"That's 4–zip," Zack said. "Have you ever been skunked before playing twenty-one?" That got Orlando fired up.

"SKUNKED? THE LITTLE MAN HAS NEVER BEEN SHUT OUT BEFORE AND HE'S NOT ABOUT TO BE NOW. EVEN THOUGH HIS BEANPOLE OPPONENT IS A FULL FOOT TALLER, HE DOESN'T STAND A CHANCE AGAINST THE OFFICIAL PLAY-BY-PLAY ANNOUNCER OF THE EVERGREEN EAGLES. WHAT WAS HIS NAME AGAIN? OR-LAN-DO. YES, THAT'S RIGHT — ORLANDO. AND WHILE YOU'RE SAYING IT, WATCH THE SMALL GUY WITH THE BIG SHOT DROP ONE IN FROM DOWNTOWN. HE PUTS IT UP OVER THE EAGLES CENTRE AND IT HITS NOTHING BUT NET. HE DOESN'T HIT THEM ALL, BUT HE GOT LUCKY WITH THAT ONE, FOLKS.

Zack looked straight past him and grinned. Orlando thought that was a strange reaction to being scored on. Then he realized they weren't alone. He spun around.

"Got room for one more in your lame game?" Megan asked, coming out of the garage.

"We've already started playing," Orlando said. "And besides, you'd never catch up." He was getting used to seeing his sister and Zack together, but when it came to hoops, he'd rather just Zack and him play.

"I'll take my chances," Megan said, flipping her blond ponytail.

"I'm okay with it, just in case you were wondering about my opinion," Zack said.

Orlando gave in. "Okay, Megan, your shot."

Zack squeezed the ball and made a bounce pass to Megan, who stood at the end of the driveway. Orlando figured she'd never beat both him and Zack and go in to score. He crouched down, spread his arms wide to stop her, and made the call.

"THERE'S NO WAY THIS IS GOING TO HAPPEN. DOESN'T THE GIRL KNOW SHE'S UP AGAINST TWO MEMBERS OF THE CHAMPION EAGLES SQUAD? SHE DRIBBLES THE BALL STRAIGHT AT HER ALL-STAR AN-NOUNCER BROTHER, THEN PASSES IT BEHIND HER BACK, LEAVING HIM ALL TWISTED UP LIKE A PRETZEL. NOW THERE'S JUST ZACK BETWEEN HER AND THE NET. THE BLOND FLASH SLOWS FOR A MOMENT TO GATHER HER STRENGTH, THEN BLOWS BY THE BIG MAN IN A SINGLE BURST, TAKING THE ROCK TO THE HOOP FOR TWO POINTS. SHE'S DONE IT AGAIN JUST LIKE SHE DID A FEW WEEKS AGO! MEGAN IS STILL QUEEN OF THE COURT!"

Zack caught the ball as it fell through the net and held it in his big hands. Orlando watched his friend, who couldn't seem to take his eyes off the shifty blue-eyed blond in the grey sweatsuit. He could see Zack wasn't upset because a girl had just turned him inside out and scored. In fact, he seemed pretty happy about it. This wasn't the super-competitive Zack he knew from the season. If it had been, the Eagles never would have been champions.

Megan darted toward Zack and stole the ball from his hands. "So, I couldn't help but notice you really picked up your play after I arrived at the game."

Zack shook his head and laughed. "I never even saw you."

"You're trying to tell me I had nothing to do with it?" Megan said in disbelief. "Then how do you explain suddenly turning into a scoring machine?"

"Easy," Zack said, pointing at Orlando. "Your brother got the whole team going. He's the only reason we won."

Megan pouted and raised her eyebrows. "The only reason?"

"Okay, and you being there, too," Zack said with a grin.

Orlando rolled his eyes. He could figure out how to pump up his teammates in the biggest game of their lives. But *this* he'd never understand.

CHECK OUT THESE OTHER BASKETBALL STORIES FROM LORIMER'S SPORTS STORIES SERIES:

Camp All-Star
by Michael Coldwell

Jeff's been invited to an elite basketball camp, and he's looking forward to some serious on-court action for two weeks straight — but Chip, his completely unserious new roommate, seems to have other ideas…

Fast Break
by Michael Coldwell

Meeting people in a new town is hard. So when Jeff runs into a group of guys who love basketball as much as he does, he makes sure to stick with them when school starts. But at school, he finds out what they're really like…

Free Throw
by Jacqueline Guest

When his mother remarries, suddenly everything changes for Matt: new school, new father, five annoying new sisters, even a smelly new dog. Worst of all, if he wants to play basketball again, he'll have to play with his old team's worst enemies.

Home Court Advantage
by Sandra Diersch

Life as a foster child can be tough — so Debbie has learned to be tough back, both at home and on the court. But when a nice couple decides to adopt her, Debbie suddenly isn't so sure of herself — and her new teammates aren't so sure about her either.

Nothing But Net
by Michael Coldwell

Playing in an out-of-town tournament can be rough, especially when you know you're the worst team on the court. But when you've got nothing to lose and a wild man like Chip Carson on your side, anything can happen…

Out of Bounds
by Sylvia Gunnery

As if it isn't bad enough that Jay's family home has been destroyed by fire, Jay has to switch schools — which means he has to choose between playing for the enemy, and not playing basketball at all. And he can't decide which is worse.

Personal Best
by Sylvia Gunnery

Jay finally gets to go to Basketball Nova Scotia Summer Camp, and he even gets to stay in a real dorm with his best friend, Mike. But Mike's older brother is also there, and he's not exactly acting like a good coach or a good big brother… .

Queen of the Court
by Michele Martin Bossley

Kallana's father has suddenly decided that joining the basketball team will be a "character-building" experience for her. But she can't dribble, she can't sink a basket, and worst of all, she will have to wear one of those hideous uniforms...

Fadeaway
by Steven Barwin

Renna's the captain of her basketball team, and is known to run a tight ship. But then a new girl from a rival team joins. Suddenly, Renna's being left out and picked on by her own teammates. Can she face this bullying and win her team back before it goes too far?

Slam Dunk
by Steven Barwin & Gabriel David Tick

The Raptors are going co-ed — which means that for the first time ever, there will be *girls* on the team. Mason's willing to see what these girls can do, but the other guys on the team aren't so sure about this...

Triple Threat
by Jacqueline Guest

When Matt's online friend, Free Throw, finally comes to Bragg Creek for a visit, the first thing they do is get a team together to compete in the summer basketball league. Unfortunately, Matt's arch-enemy has had the same idea...

Game Face
by Sylvia Gunnery

Jay's back in Rockets territory after playing for a rival team last year, and not everyone on the basketball team is welcoming him home. When Jay beats out former best friend and MVP Colin for team captain, the tension threatens to rip the team apart.

Jump Ball
by Adrienne Mercer

Basketball is more than just a game for Abby, it's everything. When her younger sister makes it onto the school basketball team, Abby can't help fighting to be the best — even if it means fighting against her own teammates.

Rebound
by Adrienne Mercer

C.J.'s just been made captain of the basketball team — but her teammate, Debi, seems determined to make C.J. miserable. Then C.J. wakes up one morning barely able to stand up. How can she show Debi up when she can't even make it onto the court?